Jayne Mackay

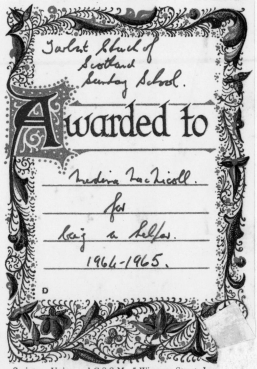

Tarbat Church of
Scotland
Sunday School.

# Awarded to

Medina MacNicoll.
for
Being a helper.
1964-1965.

D

Scripture Union and C.S.S.M., 5 Wigmore Street, Lon

Osta St

Street Balinto

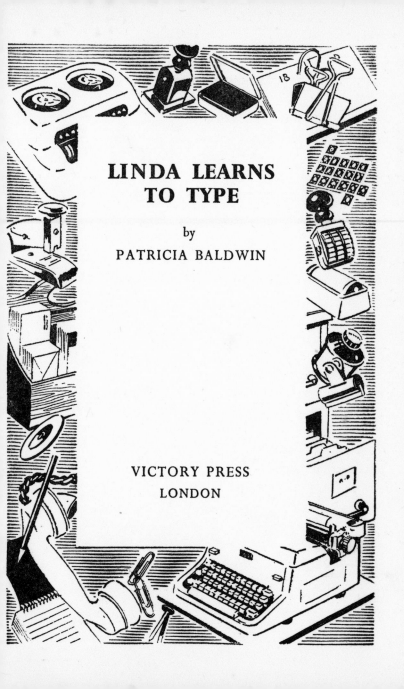

# LINDA LEARNS TO TYPE

by

PATRICIA BALDWIN

VICTORY PRESS
LONDON

*Printed in Great Britain for*
*Victory Press (Evangelical Publishers Ltd.)*
*Clapham Crescent, London, SW4, by*
*Richard Clay and Company, Ltd., Bungay, Suffolk.*

# CHAPTER ONE

"Linda, you must be mad!" Pamela Bookham said with disgust. "Do you realise that I have just offered you two tickets for the Barn Dance tomorrow night at the Social Centre and you have refused them?"

"Of course I realise," Linda Lewis replied quietly. "I just don't want to go to the Barn Dance, that's all." She turned and looked out of the window while Pamela faced the other girls in the form.

"Did you hear that?" she asked them, "Professor Lewis doesn't want to go to the Barn Dance, 'that's all,'" she mocked.

"Huh, who does she think she is?" another girl joined in. "I'd say she was getting a bit too big for her boots, if you ask me. Either that, or she's got a boy friend!"

Linda blushed and took no notice. So many of the girls at Morton Secondary Modern School lived as if they didn't know what it meant to be ambitious.

Gently she let her fingers rest on the typewriter in front of her. In a few minutes Miss Hurst would come and there would be another speed test in typing. Linda badly wanted to do well and pass her exams so that one day she could become a private secretary.

The door opened and Miss Hurst entered.

"Come along, don't waste any time," she began as the girls took their places as if the whole day lay before them.

"We will loosen up to a tune on the gramophone first, and follow that with a speed test," she said. She crossed to a gramophone on a table at the top of the room. "Everyone fit a sheet of paper and a backing sheet into her machine," she told them. "And don't forget to leave a margin and set your line spacer for double spacing."

She turned to face them.

"Hurry up, Pamela," she said. "Let out your paper release and get that sheet straight," she told her and Pamela sighed audibly.

"Now I want you to take special care of your capital letters to-day, there are several proper names in the piece I shall read."

She started the gramophone and a gentle rhythm filled the room to help the girls develop a steady, even speed. Then Miss Hurst began to read and the room was filled with the clatter of the machines.

Linda took it calmly and easily. She loved the work. Three years earlier she had taken her eleven-plus and failed miserably and felt as if the bottom had dropped out of her world. But when she had been at the Secondary School for only a year a commercial course had been introduced and Linda had thrown herself into it with enthusiasm. She was short and had dark hair and a quiet nature, but underneath she longed to get on and do well.

The first part of the lesson over, they prepared for the speed test. Like the others Linda was fifteen and knew she would be able to leave at the end of the school year, but it was no good leaving until her work was reasonably fast and accurate. Her ultimate aim was to reach 120 words per minute in shorthand and fifty words per minute in typing, but she had a long way to go. Up to now she had reached sixty words in shorthand and only thirty in typing, but if only she could reach eighty words per minute in shorthand and thirty-five in typing, she could leave and work up her speed at home or at night school.

"Are you ready?" she heard Miss Hurst ask and she shut her eyes for a moment to try to prevent herself becoming tense and awkward. "I shall take the test at a speed of thirty-five words a minute, as you ought to be working for your first certificate," Miss Hurst went on, setting her stop watch. "Five mistakes are allowed but, don't forget, if you get lost, go on from where I have reached; it's no good trying to catch up."

At last it was over and Linda smiled to herself. She had not done badly at all. Admittedly she had made fourteen mistakes, but she had finished at the right time and she felt the mistakes would disappear with practice.

The typing test was followed by a shorthand test and again Linda did well, reaching seventy-three words to the minute with very few errors.

"Practice, practice, practice!" she murmured to herself as she put her things away. The drudgery of learning was over and the rest was up to her.

She left the form-room with the others and they chattered away together as they collected their things from the cloakroom.

"Sure you don't want those tickets?" Pamela asked her as she passed.

"No thanks," she replied briefly.

Sheila Purdom, another of her form, crossed to her side.

"You ought to have some relaxation, you know," she began rather shyly. "Would you like to come to the Friday Club at the Chapel with Carol and me?"

Linda smiled.

"Everyone seems very interested in me all of a sudden," she said. "It's nice of you to ask me, Sheila, but I'd rather not. My kid sister, Mary, goes down there, but I'm afraid I'm not one for a lot of religion. I believe I can get on in the world by honest effort on my part and I should only be wasting my time if I kept going to church."

Sheila looked disappointed.

"I'm sorry you feel like that," she said and added, as Linda walked away, "Let me know if you change your mind."

Linda walked down to the bus stop feeling happy and contented, she could hardly wait to tell her family how well she was getting on. A bus drew up for Hillside Estate and she climbed in and sat by the window, but scarcely saw what they were passing.

Her father was a fitter in a nearby factory and Linda dreamed of the day when he would be able to tell his friends proudly of his daughter's achievements. Perhaps they would even be able to leave the council estate and have a small house of their own one day. Or perhaps she would be able to buy a washing machine and other luxuries for her mother to make her life easier and save her spending three mornings a week working at a nearby laundry to pay for the T.V. and other extras.

She thought of George, her brother, who at nineteen

worked at a large garage as a motor mechanic and did relief on the pumps when they were busy. He had once been full of talk about owning his own garage, but recently he had gone around with a number of fellows who spent every penny as they received it, and Linda had heard no more about his ambitious plans.

Then there was Mary with curly black hair and a ready smile. Linda bit her lip as she thought of her. Mary was pretty and did everything well and the family were always loud in her praise. She had passed her eleven-plus and was now doing well at the Grammar School, and Linda found it hard not to mind.

The bus left the main road and entered the estate where they lived. Linda looked around at the neat rows of houses where everything was so much the same and where the families all knew each other and generally got on well together. As she rose from her seat she vowed in her heart that she intended to be different and break away and make a good job of her life.

Hurrying up the path, she let herself in at the back door, eager once more to tell of the improvement in her tests. She washed her hands at the kitchen sink and hastily tidied her hair before entering the living-room to join the others.

"Do you know?" she began, but her mother interrupted her.

"Mary has some wonderful news to tell you, Linda," she said eagerly. "Go on, Mary, dear."

"You tell her," Mary replied with a smile.

"Oh, all right," her mother replied. "Linda, our Mary is getting a prize! There, what do you think of that?"

Before Linda had time to reply her brother joined in.

"You wait till Dad knows. She came home with a printed invitation for Mum and Dad to go to the Speech Day and watch her go up in front of the whole school to get her reward."

Linda muttered her congratulations before George went on:

"Pretty good, isn't it? It has taken a long time for any of us to achieve something," he said with a laugh, "but Mary has done it at last."

"And it won't be the last time," Mrs Lewis went on, glowing with pride. "What she's done once she'll do again. Can I get you some more to eat, Mary?" she finished.

Mary laughed.

"What a fuss over one small prize," she said good-naturedly, and Linda looked up quickly as if her sister had put into words her own thoughts. It was no good mentioning her small achievement now, so she ate her tea in silence. She tried to be herself when they washed up, but when she settled down to work afterwards, it was no good. Over and over again her mind wandered back to Mary and her prize, and all her bitterness at failing to gain a place at the Grammar School returned.

Shutting her books she slipped out quietly and wandered down the road. She might as well admit that she was burning with jealousy; jealousy of her own sister, and she was ashamed of herself.

Rounding a corner she scarcely noticed a figure bent over a brand new motor bike until a voice stopped her.

"What's up, Linda? Things looking black?"

She turned as Peter Johnson stood up, wiping the sweat from his forehead with the back of his hand.

"Hallo, Pete," she greeted him half-heartedly, giving him the name she had called him since they walked along to the Primary School together.

"Well, don't you like it?" he asked her and indicated the machine. "I'll take you for a ride when I have passed my test."

Linda forgot her woes and began to take interest.

"It's a beauty," she said. "When did you get it?"

"Last week," Peter replied. "I've been saving for it ever since I was old enough to do a paper round, and my folk gave me the last few pounds for my sixteenth birthday." He pulled out his handkerchief and polished the lamp as he spoke. "Mind you," he added, "I'm going to pay them back. I want it to be my very own, bought by my own effort."

Linda laughed as she remembered her words to Sheila, and then, somehow, it all came out about her tests and Mary's prize and her bitterness over it all.

"I'm sorry, Pete," she finished. "I don't know why I should bother you with all my troubles, you just happen to be the sort of fellow a girl can confide in."

"Don't apologise," he said sympathetically. "For some reason both you and I have the same urge to achieve something and, you know, we'll do it some day."

"By our own efforts," Linda laughed. "If I had persuaded Dad to send me to some posh secretarial college for nine months and cost him more than a hundred pounds in doing so I would always feel I owed him something. At least I have only myself to thank if I make the grade—or blame if I fail," she added.

"You won't fail," Peter encouraged her. "And if you do you will have me to reckon with," he added, turning back to his motor bike while Linda made her way home and settled down to some hard work with her old enthusiasm.

# CHAPTER TWO

As day followed day, Linda felt a growing desire to leave school and take a job. If she could only do well enough she could be earning and helping with expenses at home in a year's time. So she practised for hours at her shorthand and typing and took a much greater interest in the other commercial subjects as well. English had always come to her easily and she enjoyed it to the full, but now even debit and credit and easy book-keeping began to lose their terrors.

Learning how to file papers was added to her subjects and she soon felt able to slip things away quickly and find them under their proper heading when wanted. She also learned how to cut a stencil ready for taking copies of anything and how to set out letters and memos in a business-like way.

When the next tests were taken Linda passed quite easily and was just being congratulated by the others when Miss Hurst sent for her.

"Ah, there you are, Linda," she greeted her as Linda re-entered the form-room with a worried look on her face.

"Have I done something wrong, Miss Hurst?" she asked nervously, thinking back to that afternoon's test and trying to think where she might have slipped up.

Miss Hurst laughed.

"No, nothing wrong at all," she said. "I wanted a talk

with you alone because I have some exciting news for you."

Linda looked at her eagerly, wondering what was coming.

"It has been obvious for some time now that you are anxious to get on in your work, Linda," Miss Hurst continued. "Perhaps you could tell me what you hope to do when you leave school?"

Linda hesitated for a minute.

"I don't just want to be a copy-typist," she began slowly, "because then I should always be under someone else." She paused a minute and the colour came into her face before she went on quickly, "I want to get to the top, Miss Hurst. To be a private secretary to one important person, and I want that person to know I can be trusted to do a good job without letting anyone down."

There was a moment's silence, while Linda looked down at the floor regretting her outburst. Then, without looking up, she asked:

"Do you think I shall succeed, Miss Hurst? If I work very hard, I mean."

She looked up to find the teacher smiling at her.

"I'm quite sure you will, Linda, and that is why I think you will like what I am going to tell you.

"The Head and I have been watching you for some time and have been making some enquiries. How would you like to have two weeks away from school working in the Public Health Office just to get the feeling of office routine?"

"Me?" Linda gasped. "But I'd love to. Do you really mean it?"

"Of course I do," Miss Hurst replied with a smile. "We hope to send each girl out for experience when she has her first certificate, and you are the first to reach that standard. When you come back you will have a much better idea of what is expected of you and we hope it will help you to go on working hard."

"Thank you," Linda mumbled and scarcely heard herself being dismissed.

Once outside school and on the way home she realised more fully what was happening. She, Linda Lewis, was off to work on Monday for two weeks, taking the next step toward the job she so much wanted.

Bursting into the kitchen at home she found her mother preparing the tea.

"Mum!" she burst out, "I'm going to the Public Health Office on Monday. Isn't it wonderful?"

Her mother turned and looked at her in amazement.

"Whatever for, dear? Are you having an injection or something?" she asked.

Linda swung off her satchel and laughed.

"I'm sorry," she said, "but I'm so excited."

The door opened and George and Mary came in.

"Whatever is all the noise about?" her brother enquired.

"I don't know," their mother replied. "Linda is about to tell us."

"Well, it's like this," Linda began. "We had our speed tests in shorthand and typing this afternoon and I managed to get my first certificate."

"Jolly good," George broke in, while Mary astonished Linda by hugging her hard.

"What speed test was that, dear?" her mother asked her calmly.

"Eighty words a minute in shorthand and thirty-five in typing," Linda explained. "But, that's not all," she went on. "Miss Hurst sent for me afterwards and told me I was to go and work in the Public Health Office next Monday to gain experience."

"Well, that is a bit of news," her mother exclaimed. "Your Dad will be pleased."

George slapped her on the shoulder.

"Good old Sis.," he congratulated her but spoilt it by adding with a laugh, "You'll have had enough after two weeks, I'll be bound."

"I'm so glad," Mary said simply and Linda saw she was flushed with pleasure.

The rest of the evening passed slowly while Linda glowed under praise and put up with her brother's teasing as well as she could. She slipped up to her room early to dream of all the future held out to her, and was about to get into bed when there was a tap on her door.

"It's me, Mary," a voice said in a whisper. "May I come in?"

"Do."

Mary came in in her dressing-gown and slippers and sat on the end of the bed.

"I just wanted to say how glad I am about the tests and the job and everything," she said quietly.

"That's nice of you," Linda replied. "Thank you very much."

Mary wriggled her feet with embarrassment and a slipper fell off with a thud on the lino.

"I wanted you to know that . . ." She hesitated before hurrying on, "that I'd been praying you would do well and you have."

"Praying?" Linda echoed. "Whatever for?"

Mary took a deep breath.

"It's like this," she explained. "At the Friday Club we hear about God and how He loved us enough to send His Son, Jesus Christ, to die on the cross for us. Well, I have thanked Him for doing that and become a Christian, which means God is my Father and will hear me if I talk to Him. So I asked Him to help you." She finished off flushed and confused and looked at her sister.

"That's very interesting I'm sure," Linda replied briefly. "But, if you want to know, I can manage all right without prayer." Her voice hardened. "I think you had better go back to bed and get some sleep and, in future, I should keep your prayers to your own affairs."

Her young sister looked at her with tears in her eyes.

"I didn't mean to make you angry," she muttered and fled from the room.

"Prayers indeed," Linda snorted as she shut the door behind her. "A lot of good prayers are likely to do me. It's hard work I need, not prayers."

She climbed into bed and soon forgot the upset as sleep came to her, and she dreamed she was in charge of a huge office with simply hundreds of girls at her command!

The following Monday morning dawned crisp and bright and Linda set off for the Public Health Office in good spirits. She whistled as she walked to the bus stop and gave a gay "Good-morning" to the conductor.

"You seem pleased with life," he said with a chuckle. "Been left a fortune, or something?"

"Not quite," Linda replied with a laugh and settled herself down on the seat beside the door, eager to tell someone how excited she felt.

She watched as the conductor made his way along the bus collecting the fares and then, when he was once more standing near her on the platform, she turned to him.

"I'm not going to school for two whole weeks," she informed him.

"And why would that be?" he enquired.

"Because I'm going to work in the Public Health Office for a fortnight to see if I like it," she replied.

He looked at her and then, after a pause, asked her:

"Do you know where it is?"

Linda hesitated.

"Sort of," she said. "It's along the main road near the Town Hall, isn't it? Why?"

"Oh, never mind," he replied. "If you're excited about it I don't suppose you'll ever notice what a dingy, draughty old place it is. They hope to rebuild it next year. All the best."

He swung round and made his way up to the top deck leaving Linda with a puzzled look on her face. She had never noticed the Public Health Office before but had imagined it to be clean and modern and living up to its name.

She shrugged her shoulders and began to get out. As if the building mattered, it was the job she wanted.

The conductor was right. When she reached her

destination she found it to be a gaunt old house and not the least bit inviting.

She pushed open the door and entered a gloomy hall with some well-polished but very old lino on the floor. There was no one about and she stood for a moment wondering whether to flee while the going was good and return to her smart modern school.

Suddenly a hatch was flung open and a girl looked out, while Linda stood feeling both stupid and awkward.

"Did you want something?" the girl enquired at last, and added to an unseen friend, "we haven't a clinic this morning, have we, Jill?"

Linda cleared her throat and crossed to the hatch.

"My name is Linda Lewis," she explained. "I was told to come here at nine o'clock this morning, to work here."

The girl looked at her hard.

"Sure it was here, dear?" she asked and Linda felt her heart sink. "Tell me again," the girl asked her and Linda explained herself in more detail.

"Do you know anything about a girl from the Sec. coming for a fortnight?" the head in the hatch asked her unseen companion, and Linda wondered what she should do.

Just then the front door opened and an older person hurried in. She looked at Linda as she took off her coat.

"Linda Lewis?" she enquired briefly and, without waiting for a reply, brushed past her and entered another room. "Follow me and I will tell you what to do."

Linda followed slowly with butterflies in her stomach.

Somehow the V.I.P. treatment she had dreamed about was missing.

"Now take off your coat and sit down," she was told. "My name is Miss Harris and you will be under me while you are here."

Linda hung her coat on the door, hoping she was doing the right thing, while Miss Harris began to sort her way rapidly through a pile of letters at a large desk in the middle of the room. This gave Linda time to look round at the filing cabinets and various tables and chairs which seemed to fill the room to capacity. There was a typewriter under its cover in the corner and a waste-paper basket spilling its contents over the hearth. There were papers everywhere and a general atmosphere of confusion.

Looking up she found she was being watched.

"It isn't quite what you expected, is it?" Miss Harris enquired with a wry smile. "And, I might add, it isn't as I should like it. I'm afraid most of you girls work to get money to spend on yourselves and it seems impossible to find anyone really keen to do well."

Linda drew in a breath to say that she was one of the few keen ones, and then decided to keep quiet and show her keenness by her actions.

After a brief outline of the office routine Miss Harris glanced at her watch and rose to her feet.

"I'm very sorry to leave you, but I have an appointment at ten a.m. Perhaps you could fill in your time looking round and seeing what the other girls do." She put on her coat. "You could make a cup of tea at eleven o'clock, too. Jill will show you where we keep the things. And if you could possibly do something about that waste-paper basket I should be delighted. You look a sensible girl."

She hurried out, leaving Linda determined to live up to her last remark.

First priority was the offending waste-paper basket and Linda crushed down its contents and picked up the assortment in the hearth. Then she stood hesitating and wondered if she could find a bin or something to empty the rubbish in. She had seen nothing in the hall, so decided to try a door at the other side of the room. Opening it slowly she found herself in a passage with two more doors at the far end. She walked to the first and opened it, but found only a wash-basin and toilet beyond, so closed it again and tried the other.

Inside the second room there were piles of papers and pamphlets and cartons of all sizes and descriptions piled high against two walls. But at the further side was another door which led to the back-yard and the dustbin.

Emptying the basket Linda returned triumphant to the office, having gained considerable confidence from her success.

For the next few minutes she went round the room reading the various charts which were hung on boards on the walls. Then, when she had been right round, she felt she ought to go through to the others.

She tapped nervously on the door.

"Come in," a voice called and she opened the door and entered.

"What, you still here?" the girl she had seen in the

hatch asked, and Linda explained once again what she was doing.

A tall, pretty girl she had not seen before came towards her from her desk near the window.

"My name is Jill Sutherland," she explained kindly. "This is Gladys—I think you two have met!"

Gladys giggled and began to sort a pile of cards she had in front of her. Linda watched her a moment and noticed that her finger nails were long and rather dirty, so she made a mental note that fingers were so obvious in office work that they must be kept immaculate at all costs.

"What are you doing?" she asked after a minute and walked round to get a better look at the cards.

"These are anti-polio registration cards," Gladys told her. "The ones I put there have had two injections and these over here only one. There is a clinic next week and I have to send out a card to everyone who has had only one injection."

"Have you been done?" Linda asked curiously.

"Oh, yes, of course," Gladys replied. "Haven't you?"

"Not yet."

This amused Gladys no end.

"You wait till Miss Harris hears that," she chuckled. "She'll have a fit! She's mad keen on everyone being 'done', as she calls it."

"There is a chart in this long drawer showing the number of cases of all the infectious diseases in the town up to last month," Jill told her, pulling open a drawer and pointing out the coloured lines denoting each disease. "And here is another one showing the different districts and where the more serious illnesses such as polio have occurred."

"How interesting," Linda exclaimed and picked up the second chart to examine it. Suddenly she let out a little gasp. "Is 'P' for polio?" she enquired.

"That's right, why?" Jill asked her.

"There's a 'P' just along the road from where I live," she said slowly, "and another at the other side of the Estate. I never knew."

"So many people only find out too late," Jill said sympathetically. "Don't worry, both those cases were last summer, but if I were you I should tell Miss Harris you have not been immunised and she will probably fit you in next week."

For Linda the following two weeks were thrilling. The office was far from modern and there were several things which she jotted in a note-book to be sure to avoid them when she eventually took charge of an office of her own. But there were other ideas which she knew she would do well to follow.

It was with great reluctance that she said goodbye to her new friends and prepared to go back to school.

"It has been a pleasure to have you, Linda," Miss Harris told her as she put on her coat.

"Thank you, Miss Harris. And thank you for being so patient with me," Linda replied as she left.

## CHAPTER THREE

Back at school, Linda worked with enthusiasm. Her short time away had given her a taste of freedom and the opportunity to make up her mind finally as to her future. After that the time flew by until she found that scarcely a month remained of her very last term at school.

One by one during that summer term, the girls who were leaving were called to the study to talk over their future. Now, at last, it was Linda's turn and she stood outside the door feeling as if she would burst with excitement.

"Come in," Miss Grimmett called in answer to her knock. "Ah, there you are, Linda. Sit down and tell me what plans you have made for when you leave."

Linda perched on a chair.

"I haven't done very much at all, yet, Miss Grimmett," she admitted. "I thought I would have a short holiday and then begin to look round."

"I asked because I didn't wish to upset any plans you may have made," Miss Grimmett said kindly. "I usually try to help each girl get off to a good start and I have one or two ideas here which you might like to follow up. It would not be necessary for you to start until you have had some time off first."

She picked up a bundle of papers from her desk.

"I don't want you to feel you must fill one of these

vacancies," she explained. "But, at least you could go along and see what the work is like."

Linda leaned forward eagerly.

"The first one is with a caravan firm. You probably know it, Mayson and Jones. They want a girl in the office with a knowledge of book-keeping as well as typing, and preferably shorthand as well."

She looked up, but Linda said nothing.

"Then there is one here from Russells the builders, wanting someone to do shorthand and typing and also willing to answer the 'phone. And a third from a partnership of chiropodists wanting a junior secretary. Well, what do you feel about those?"

"I don't know," Linda replied slowly. "They really aren't the kind of work I had in mind, but I could always go and see."

"I think you would be wise to do so," the Head agreed. "After all, experience is the thing you need first of all, Linda. Climbing to the top of the tree takes time."

"Yes, Miss Grimmett," Linda agreed, trying not to show her disappointment.

"There are several things you ought to know about applying for a post. First of all you should type out a sheet giving your full name and address, your age and education and your qualifications. Also, you must remember to ask what the job entails—the hours of work, whether you are expected to work on a Saturday and, of course, the salary you are offered."

A brief smile crossed Linda's face as she listened.

"Then there is another important thing," the Head continued. "You must be quite definite about whether you intend to take the job offered to you or not. Either say 'yes' if you are absolutely certain or, of course, turn it down at once if you feel it is impossible. But, if you are not sure, then ask if you may let your interviewer know in, say, three days' time and be sure to do so."

Linda nodded agreement.

"Thank you, Miss Grimmett," she said. "Meanwhile I shall go on practising."

"Oh, yes, do," the Head replied. "And another thing which will always stand you in good stead; try to cultivate the habit of reading—not silly stories, but interesting, well-written books about real people doing helpful and adventurous things."

Linda left the study clutching the papers on which were the details of the various jobs. She was just longing to start work, but what a selection! She smiled grimly as she thought of them, caravans, bricks and feet! Feet, of all things!

However, once back in the form-room she made several copies of her own particulars and wrote away to apply for all three.

At home she said very little. She could just imagine the remarks her brother would pass if he heard about the different jobs she was after.

The appointments came at last and Linda again saw Miss Grimmett and asked her permission to be away from school to keep them. She had given each prospective employer a different time on the same day and they had fitted in with very little alteration.

"What on earth are you doing dressed up like that?" her brother asked her when the day came and she went down to breakfast in a crisp cotton frock instead of her school things.

"Never you mind," she said grimly and waited until he had gone off to work.

"Tell me, now he's gone," Mary urged her with a laugh. "Are you going somewhere special?"

Linda saw her father look over the top of his paper and listen.

"As a matter of fact I am," she said at last. "Mum knows all about it and I suppose the rest of you will know soon. I am going for three interviews about different jobs."

Her father smiled.

"It will be rather difficult to hold down three jobs at once, won't it?" he asked innocently.

"Don't be silly, Dad," Linda burst out. "I knew you would tease me if I told you. Of course I shan't take three at once. Anyway, I probably won't take any of them."

Her father put his hand affectionately on her arm.

"I'm only teasing, dear," he said. "I hope very much that you will find a good job and be very happy."

"Do tell me what the different jobs are, Linda," Mary asked. "It is all so exciting."

Linda looked at her young sister and felt her own enthusiasm return.

"One is at Mayson and Jones, the caravan people, and another at Russells the builders," she told them.

"And the third?" Mary pressed her.

"The third is for some chiropodists," Linda replied in a

matter-of-fact voice and a smile crossed her face as her
father gave a hearty laugh.

At exactly 10.45 a.m. Linda knocked on the office door
at Mayson and Jones.

"Come in," a voice called and she entered and found
herself facing a very large man with his tie flapping loosely
round his open collar and a cigar in his hand.

"Good morning," Linda murmured.

"Ah, you'll be Linda Lewis, I expect," the large man
greeted her and swept round the office to pull out a chair
for her. "You look very young, if I may say so, but very
pretty," he added and gave a laugh which made Linda
flush with anger. "Now, let me see, you say you can type
and do shorthand and um . . . ah, book-keeping as well.
I think we should get on splendidly. When can you
start?"

Linda looked at him in astonishment. He hadn't asked
her anything at all and she felt she couldn't possibly work
for such an unpleasant man. What had Miss Grimmett
said, "If you know it is impossible, say so." But she
daren't. Something about this man told her he could be
as angry as he could be sugary, so she played for time.

"I'm afraid I shall have to let you know," she stammered. "I mean, I have another interview to-day and
then I shall decide and let you know to-morrow." She
rose to her feet and waited for him to say something but
he remained silent until she reached the door and said
"Good morning." Then he barked at her:

"Good morning. And mind you shut the door behind
you."

With a sigh of relief Linda hurried away and set off in

the direction of Russells. She had some time in hand, so slipped into a coffee bar on her way to steady her nerves.

Arriving at length at the builder's yard, she looked around until she saw the offices and a large notice pointing to "Enquiries". The door said, "Walk In, Please", so she did so, and tapped on a sliding glass panel inside. It opened and a well-groomed young lady in her early twenties looked out.

"Can I help you?" she asked in a highly efficient way, and Linda explained why she had come.

"Just one moment, please." The panel slammed back and Linda heard the murmur of voices. Then a door opened and the young lady came out. "Would you come this way, please, Miss Lewis," she said.

Linda swallowed hard and tried not to giggle and then suddenly felt very unpolished and young in comparison with the efficient young lady ahead.

"Mr Wetherall will ring a buzzer twice when he is ready to see you," she was told as she was ushered into a gleaming waiting-room.

On the walls were pictures of various exotic modern buildings each with the inscription, "Erected by Russells in the year . . ." Linda looked at them and the polished leather chairs and was about to sit gingerly on the edge of one of the chairs when the buzzer rang loudly just above her head and she leapt to her feet in fright.

"Miss Lewis?" An immaculate gentleman greeted her as she entered an adjoining room. He rose to his feet until she had seated herself in a chair he indicated, and looked her up and down through his rimless spectacles.

"Now let me see, Miss Lewis," he began. "You are

C

sixteen and hold your R.S.M. certificate for eighty words per minute shorthand and thirty-five words per minute typing. Is that correct?"

"Yes, sir," Linda replied in a whisper.

"Speak up then, and let us get this matter settled," he told her. "Can you use a switchboard?"

The question was so sudden that for a moment Linda was taken by surprise.

"You mean a telephone switchboard?" she enquired nervously.

"Naturally," he replied briefly.

"I haven't used one, but I could soon learn," she told him.

"A pity. I distinctly stated in my advertisement that we needed help on the telephone." He stood up and Linda realised it was all over.

She hurried from the room and out of the building.

Of all the horrid experiences, she thought. One employer all gushing and the other ice cold—and she had only "feet" left. The very thought of it revolted her and, on the spur of the moment, she found a telephone kiosk, looked up the number, and rang to say she could not take the post.

"Oh, I am so sorry," a kind voice answered her. "After your nice letter we were all looking forward to having you with us. Well, I'm sure we all hope you find a pleasant job which will make you really happy. Goodbye."

The 'phone clicked and Linda looked at it.

"Bother!" she said out loud. "That person sounded a dear."

She flounced out of the 'phone box feeling angry with herself and caught a bus home to tell her family.

# CHAPTER FOUR

T̶HAT afternoon Linda was at a loss to know what to
do with herself. She was annoyed at what she con-
sidered to be her failure that morning and very anxious
about what Miss Grimmett would say when she knew.

Half-heartedly she began to practise her shorthand, but
everything seemed to go wrong and, after a while, she
picked up the local paper and scanned the Situations
Vacant column.

Suddenly she drew in her breath and spread the paper
on the dining-table to read it better. There, half way
down the page, was an advertisement which made her
tingle.

Wanted, keen young lady with knowledge of shorthand
and typing, in small family chocolate firm [it ran].
Excellent prospects for promotion for the right
applicant. Apply in writing, giving full particulars to
Stapletons, 593, Turner's Lane, and mark the envelope
TYP.

Linda leaped to her feet and ran upstairs to find her
pen and a copy of her particulars and qualifications. Then,
grabbing a writing pad, she settled herself at the dining-
table, wrote a covering letter in her neatest handwriting,
and enclosed a stamped, addressed envelope for a reply.
She was about to stamp her own letter when she had an

idea, and, glancing in the mirror to see that she was tidy, she fetched her bicycle from the shed where it was kept and set off in the direction of Turner's Lane.

The very next morning her envelope flopped on the mat with a reply. Linda picked it up and was scarcely able to open it for excitement.

It was all right, the job was not filled and she was to go for an interview at 2.15 p.m. that very afternoon.

Miss Grimmett was very kind when Linda told her what had happened and willingly gave her permission to keep her new appointment. It was with high hopes that she again made her way to Turner's Lane and up to the main building at Stapletons.

Once inside the office Linda found herself facing an elderly gentleman with steel-grey hair and kindly eyes.

"Do sit down," he told her, and the way he said it dispelled Linda's fears at once.

"You must understand from the start that I was expecting someone older than you, my dear," Mr Stapleton explained in a fatherly way. "But seeing you have replied so promptly and are evidently so keen, the least we can do is to give you a fair interview."

He then talked to Linda for a few minutes about the weather and other things to set her at ease before getting down to business.

"I like to interview all prospective employees myself when possible," he told her. "You see, this really is a family concern and I think everyone should know me personally and not think of me as someone shut away and unapproachable.

"Tell me now," he said suddenly, "have you any hobbies?"

"Er . . . not really, sir," Linda stammered. "I spend a lot of my time practising my shorthand."

"No tennis, or anything like that?" he went on.

"Only at school," Linda admitted.

"That's a pity. Everyone ought to have a hobby to relax them. Now mine is colour photography and I get enormous fun out of it. But it doesn't matter what it is, sailing or crosswords, it gives you a break."

Linda made a mental note that she had already come down on one point.

"Tell me about your home," Mr Stapleton went on next and Linda found herself telling him all about her family and their various occupations.

"Are you a church-going family?" was his next question.

Linda looked up quickly.

"No, we hardly ever go," she said. "That is, except Mary, my young sister, she goes quite a bit."

"It's a funny thing that the youngest in a family can turn out to be the wisest," Mr Stapleton commented quietly, and Linda wondered what he could mean.

"Well now," Mr Stapleton said, rising to his feet. "I like your keenness, Linda, and I think you mean to do well. I'm going to hand you over to my personal secretary, Miss Cornell, now and see what she thinks of your qualifications."

To Linda's astonishment, she was kept at the factory for most of the afternoon. Miss Cornell gave her typing and shorthand tests, questioned her thoroughly about filing, book-keeping and stencilling, and then set her a short test in English with a few tricky words for her to spell.

Last of all she had a letter to compose and type out in a business-like manner and then Miss Cornell turned to her and smiled.

"Well," she said. "Have I put you off completely with such an ordeal?"

"No, not at all," Linda admitted. "It was rather fun after the first few minutes, but I'm afraid I haven't done very well." She looked at the older woman expectantly.

"You're a little bit slow in some things," Miss Cornell agreed. "Now I am going to give you the hardest test of all."

"What is that?" Linda asked with a puzzled expression.

"I expect you have dreamed wonderful dreams as your time to go out to work has come nearer, haven't you? Well, I'm going to ask you to forget your dreams and come in to the factory at the bottom of the typing pool." She held up her hand as Linda was about to speak. "If you are willing to practise and, if necessary, go along to night school, then I promise you will only be at the bottom a short while before you begin to climb. If you work hard, who knows, you may step into my shoes one day?"

"I'll practise like anything," Linda assured her. "I like it here and you and Mr Stapleton have been so kind to me. I'm sure I would rather work my way up happily here than start higher in a job which did not interest me."

And so it turned out that Linda returned home

practically dancing for joy, all ready to start work ten days after term ended.

The news soon spread among the neighbours and before long Peter stood at the door wanting to know more and offering his congratulations.

"I can take you for a spin on my bike now," he told her. "I've passed my test and am just longing for an excuse for a run out."

So they went off together and it set the seal to a really happy day for Linda.

Time passed quickly after that, during which Linda took down radio talks in shorthand, battered away on a borrowed typewriter and spent most evenings being whisked away to local beauty-spots on the back of Peter's motor bicycle.

Alone in her room at night her thoughts roamed over a host of subjects from how high she would climb up the tree of success to Mr Stapleton's remark about Mary. Why should a successful man like that say her young sister was wise just because she went to church? Perhaps one day she would be in a position to ask him, but meanwhile she began to respect Mary a little more for her unwavering love for her Bible and regular attendance both at the Friday Club and also at church on Sundays. It certainly seemed to keep her pleasant to live with if it did nothing else.

At long last Linda entered the gates of the chocolate factory once more and this time she belonged. School was over and her new life about to begin.

It was all so new she scarcely knew which way she was taken until she realised someone was talking to her.

"Hallo, are you the new one?" a pleasant voice asked. "My name is Joan Fraser."

"I'm Linda Lewis."

"Good. Now we know each other. If you keep near me I will show you the ropes and help you out if you are muddled by anything."

"Thank you very much," Linda said with real gratitude.

They entered quite a large room where several girls worked together.

"This is the typists' pool," Joan explained. "We all stay here and do whatever work comes through and then, if all goes well, some of us will be moved out to become junior secretaries and then full secretaries to one of the department heads."

Miss Cornell approached them.

"Hallo, Linda. I see Joan has taken you under her wing," she greeted them. "I want you to have a good look round for a day or two to see what is going on and then you will be ready to take your place with the others. If you get in a muddle and Joan cannot sort you out, then come up to me and I will see what I can do."

"Thank you, Miss Cornell," Linda replied and was just thinking what a happy office it appeared to be when a dark-haired, untidy-looking girl at a nearby desk dug her in the ribs as she passed and hissed:

"We don't want any favourites here. And if you will take my advice you'll keep away from Joan Fraser—she's religious!"

# CHAPTER FIVE

IT took Linda several days to "find her feet". First of all she was taken right through the factory, where she watched with interest as great baths of chocolate were swirled and mixed for days on end. It was necessary for her to know exactly where to find each department and learn the names of the managers and secretaries so that she would know where to go when there were things to distribute.

Also she had to master the intricacies of the post. Every letter that came to the factory or was sent out had to go through the Post Room, where it was sorted and a record kept of its arrival or dispatch.

Then there was a great deal going on in the typist pool itself, and gradually she was drawn into the life of the firm. At first she was sent on simple messages and put in charge of the cups of tea they all had at 10.30 a.m. Then she spent a whole afternoon folding invoices and putting them into addressed envelopes.

"Linda," Miss Cornell called one day when she had been there just over a month, "Linda, I want to add to your duties now. You seem to be nicely settled, so I am going to give you one or two things for which you will be responsible."

"Thank you, Miss Cornell," Linda said with a smile of pleasure.

"When you arrive in the morning I want you to be responsible for the mail on your own. Tessa Mayhew has been doing it up to now, but she can take over the production and wage charts. All you have to do is go to the Post Room, and you will be given the mail after it has been recorded. Bring it up here and sort it out, and then take it round to the various departments."

"Yes, Miss Cornell," Linda agreed.

"In the late afternoon," Miss Cornell went on, "you will again go round the departments and collect the letters for the outgoing mail and take them to the Post Room. Do you understand?"

"Yes, thank you, Miss Cornell. Will you tell Tessa?"

"Oh, yes, I'll tell her, don't you worry."

Linda was about to go when she was called back.

"I think you could type out a few letters now, too. I will give you one or two when I give the work out to the others."

"Oh, thank you, Miss Cornell," Linda replied and went and sat down at her desk.

The letters proved more difficult than Linda had imagined could be possible. She typed the first and was feeling very pleased with herself when Joan came and looked over her shoulder.

"I'm afraid you'll have to do that again, won't you?" she said.

"But why?" Linda asked in astonishment. "It's all right, isn't it?"

"It's not bad at all," Joan said kindly, "but if you look carefully you will see the middle paragraph somehow has treble spacing in the middle of it. That will never do."

"But no one would notice that," Linda objected.

"I noticed it," Joan said with a laugh. "I know it seems hard, Linda, but you must remember that letters are a firm's ambassadors and must be perfect. A letter must be business-like, no chatty parts mixed in and no mistakes."

Linda pulled a wry face.

"I know you're right," she agreed. "It just seems a pity!"

She fitted another sheet and typed with great care.

"That comes of showing Miss Clever-Sticks your work," a voice said behind her, and Linda turned to find Tessa grinning at her from her desk near by. "If you take my advice you'll keep your work to yourself and push it in with the other finished things when it is done. Otherwise you will spend all your time re-doing things which have very little wrong with them."

"But it did have something wrong with it," Linda objected.

"Nothing to make a song about," Tessa insisted. "You get on my nerves with all your wonderful ideas and desire to please everyone."

Linda was about to reply when she remembered her father once saying that to make a job go smoothly it was essential for everyone to make a point of getting on well together.

So she kept quiet although she could not help comparing Tessa and Joan as she continued typing the offending letter again. Tessa was so untidy and slovenly and her tongue was so sharp whereas Joan always kept herself so smart and fresh and if she were religious, at least she lived it out in her life by being kind and considerate to the others.

The longer Linda stayed in the office the more frequently she found her thoughts wandering to the different types of girls with whom she worked. Most of them were decent ordinary girls who did a good job and remained almost unnoticed. But Joan and Tessa were different. She found it hard to express her thoughts, but, if she had to do so, she would have said that Joan seemed to radiate helpfulness and cheerfulness while Tessa did just the opposite.

After some time had passed Linda was given yet another job to do and this time it was to sort out the various order forms for different areas of the country and overseas. She was surprised how far Stapletons chocolates travelled and had a feeling of pride as she read New York, Toronto, Geneva and other far-away places on the papers in front of her.

"Buck up, Linda," Tessa said, coming up to her. "Those have all to be finished before we go. It's no good going all dreamy-eyed about all the place-names you read. I can assure you we shall never visit any of them."

"You never know," Linda countered. "By the way, can you tell me where this one is to go, it's smudged right across the name and I can't read it."

"Just shove it in anywhere," Tessa told her, shrugging her shoulders. "Someone else can have the headache of sorting it out later."

"I can't do that," Linda said, getting to her feet. "I shall have to ask Miss Cornell."

"Oh, don't be soppy," Tessa taunted her. "You will

have the lot of us held up if you do that and I have a date to-night."

"I'm sorry," Linda apologised. "I'll make a point of asking Miss Cornell to excuse you on the dot of 5.30 p.m." She swung on her heel, wondering how long her patience would last. "After all, we are paid to do the job," she couldn't resist adding and left Tessa fuming as she went to find Miss Cornell.

As it turned out, the work was done in good time and, not only was Tessa able to keep her date, but Linda was able to go for another spin on the back of Peter's motor bike.

"How's the job?" he asked her as they left the bike and walked to a high point nearby for a good view of the district.

"Fine, thanks. It all seemed a muddle at first but now things are sorting themselves out and I am not feeling so strange."

They talked for a while before making their way back.

"It makes a lovely change coming out like this," Linda told him and he turned as if to speak. "Were you about to say something?" she asked as he remained silent.

He laughed.

"You old thought-reader!" he said. "As a matter of fact I was. It's just that I'm afraid I can't come out to-morrow; I have a lecture I must attend. And, well, I can't come out on Saturday, either, I've promised Dad I will give him a hand."

"Gardening, or something?" Linda asked, trying not to show her disappointment.

"No, decorating. Mum has been going on about the

hall and staircase ever since she did the spring cleaning, so Dad promised he would make a start on Saturday and have the place all nice for the winter."

"I see." Linda climbed on the back of the bike and hung on. "Oh well, I shall have to find something else to do," she told him before her words were lost in the roar of the engine.

Linda forgot her disappointment in the rush of work the next morning, but, as she ate her midday meal, she thought about Saturday and tried to think of something pleasant to do.

"Feeling blue?" Joan asked her, coming up and putting her things at the same table.

"I am rather," Linda admitted with a laugh.

"Can I help in any way? Is it something at work?"

"No, nothing at all," Linda replied. "I expect you'll think I'm rather silly if I tell you."

"I'm sure I won't," her friend assured her. "Of course, if you would rather not say anything let's talk about something else."

But Linda was glad to talk and told her all about Peter and the fun they had together and finished up by telling her about her disappointment over Saturday.

"It all sounds rather silly to talk about it!" she finished. "It's just that the weather is so lovely for the time of year and, well, I like going out with Peter."

Joan nodded sympathetically.

"I'm going out with the young people from the Friday Club on Saturday," she said slowly. "Do you think you would like to come with us?"

She looked at Linda who remained quiet.

"Let me tell you a bit more about us," she went on. "I believe your young sister Mary comes to the Friday Club, doesn't she?"

Linda nodded.

"She is in one of the middle groups," Joan told her. "The older group is called the Super Seniors and the members are fifteen to twenty-five years of age. We have a Bible Study each Friday evening and then most Saturdays we all get together and do something special.

"This week we are going for a bicycle ride and finishing up with a picnic and chat together. I suppose about ten or a dozen fellows and girls will turn up and our leaders, Mr and Mrs Chandler. How about it?"

"It sounds great," Linda admitted. "But, well . . . I don't know."

"Don't say the come-down to a pedal bike is too much for you!" Joan teased her.

"Of course not," Linda assured her quickly. "It's just that it is rather butting in on your fun, isn't it?"

"Not at all. The others wouldn't mind a bit, really they wouldn't. In fact Mr and Mrs Chandler ask us to bring our friends."

Linda thought for a minute, wondering what she might be letting herself in for.

"O.K.," she said, making up her mind. "I'll come, but I hope none of you will preach at me!"

"You wouldn't come to any harm!" her friend replied with a mischievous smile.

# CHAPTER SIX

FRIDAY was always a busy day, with the office to clear up at the end of the week, and Linda worked hard, eager to get away and tackle some of the things she normally did on a Saturday morning. Everything had gone well and they were all tidying away their typewriters when Miss Cornell hurried into the room with a stack of papers in her hand.

"I'm very sorry, everyone," she began, "but there is some urgent work here that we simply must do to-night. The financial statement from the accountant has been held up and only just come through and we must have copies in the hands of the shareholders on Monday morning ready for the Annual General Business Meeting."

She glanced at the clock.

"I see it is time for you to go so I am going to ask for volunteers to complete this task either to-night or to-morrow morning."

Everyone looked at everyone else, but Joan was the only one to say anything.

"I'll do them, Miss Cornell," she said willingly.

Miss Cornell continued to look at the other girls.

"Are you going to let Joan do them on her own?" she asked, and Linda hurried forward from her desk.

"If it's anything I can do I don't mind staying," she offered.

No one else made any move and Miss Cornell sighed.

"Well, it looks as if you two will be doing the job on your own," she said apologetically. "The rest of you may go now."

For a few moments there was a clattering and a scraping while the other girls put their things away and went out, and then Joan and Linda moved on to the big table at the top of the room and began to work with a will.

"It's just a matter of folding the balance sheets tidily, putting them in the envelopes and stamping them," Miss Cornell explained to Linda. "Joan will use the addressograph and hand the envelopes to you."

She turned to Joan.

"Here is the list for you to check the addresses. I hope it won't take you too long."

As it turned out it took them until very nearly seven o'clock, and Linda was getting anxious about her mother.

"You must explain that you will be late sometimes," Joan told her. "After all, if you are going to be anything of a secretary then your work must come before your leisure. If Miss Cornell had asked us to come in to-morrow, we should have come."

"What, and miss the picnic?" Linda asked in astonishment.

"Why not? Picnics come fairly frequently, but it is only rarely that urgent work comes in and makes it necessary for anyone to work overtime. It may happen several times in a week or two and then not again for months, you can never tell."

"I suppose you are right," Linda agreed, tidying up her

D

things and looking at the bundles of letters. "Shall I post these or what do we do with them?"

"I'll take them. I pass the P.O. on my way and I can put them in my bicycle saddlebag to take them down."

They made their way downstairs and Linda helped her friend pack in the letters securely.

"See you to-morrow," she said as she left her.

"Cheerio! Ten-thirty sharp, outside the chapel," Joan called after her, "and don't forget your food!"

At exactly half-past ten the following morning, Linda shyly approached a group of young people near the chapel not very far from her home. She looked round anxiously for Joan and her friend was ready for her, and very soon she forgot her shyness and was chattering away merrily to the others.

"Why, hallo!" she said in surprise as a familiar face approached. "Sheila Purdom, and Carol, too. I'd clean forgotten you might be here!"

At last they were all ready and the long stream of bicycles took their places ready to go. Linda looked at them and knew she was going to enjoy herself; but there was something she could not understand at all. Everyone got on so well with everyone else! Unlike the crowds she had been with on previous occasions, there was no back-biting and cattiness or remarks passed about each other. They were all so happy and gay.

They moved off and pedalled along for some time into the open country and then, sweeping over hill and dale, they at last descended a long hill to a road by a river bank. Here the leaders slowed down and then ambled

those who help themselves," their leader continued. "Take the story of the feeding of the five thousand, for instance. God blessed the food to feed the multitude, but it was the disciples who had to produce the food and hand it round and clear up afterwards. God will do the part we cannot do. There is the story of Peter in prison; God opened the gates and made the chains fall off, but it was Peter who was told to put on his own sandals. Do you see what I am getting at?"

"Yes, sir. I'd never thought of that. In the first miracle, Jesus turned the water into wine but the servants had to fill the pots and hand it round."

"That's the idea. Time and again we find examples like that. Jesus raised Lazarus, but the people around unwrapped him."

"And it's the same with becoming a Christian," Mrs Chandler broke in. "So many people think they can live good lives and earn salvation, but it isn't that at all. God in His mercy sent His Son to die for our sins at Calvary. He has done His part, but it will do us no good at all if we will not believe in Him and take the definite decision to live out that belief and let God have control of our lives."

"Yes," her husband agreed. "Our lovely old verse, John iii, 16, illustrates that exactly. 'For God so loved the world, that He gave His only begotten Son', that is God's part, and then comes ours, 'That whosoever believeth in Him should not perish, but have everlasting life'."

He turned to Richard again.

"Have I answered your question for you, Dick?" he asked.

"Yes, thanks. And you have given me lots to think about, too," Richard replied, echoing the thoughts of them all.

Linda continued to think about all she had heard on the way home and in the evening, too. Perhaps after all the Friday Club could offer her something in life, something she didn't understand as yet, but which appeared to make such a difference in the lives of her new friends.

# CHAPTER SEVEN

MONDAY began badly for Linda. To begin with she overslept and had to snatch a bite of breakfast before running down the road in time to see the bus draw away without her. She was annoyed with herself for dropping off to sleep again after she had been called and it did nothing to cheer her up to watch the bus disappear in the distance.

Hurrying along a footpath she eventually caught a bus on the main road and puffed her way into the office a good five minutes late.

"Mr Stapleton will want the post in good time this morning—he has a busy day in front of him," Miss Cornell told her, and gave a meaning look at the clock.

"I'm afraid I missed my bus," Linda explained briefly and hurried out of the room and down to the Post Room where the letters were all ready for her.

She picked them up and soon had them in the various departments and then made her way back to the typists' General Office.

"I'm afraid Mr Stapleton is not in yet," Tessa was saying as she entered. "So sorry, goodbye."

"But Mr Stapleton is in," Linda assured her angrily. "Why did you say he was not?"

"Don't be silly," Tessa replied sarcastically. "You don't honestly think I was going over to find out, do you?" She turned to the girl next to her and ignored Linda.

"Where's Joan this morning?" Linda asked suddenly, realising her friend was missing.

"She was sent for to go somewhere. Now go away and stop cross-examining me," Tessa bit back.

Linda crossed to her desk and sat down. Everything was going wrong this morning. First she was late and then Tessa letting the firm down like that on the 'phone, and Joan—where was Joan?

Half-heartedly she started copying a high pile of order sheets which Miss Cornell had left on her desk for her. But she made several mistakes and had to re-do a number of forms.

Joan came back into the room shortly before dinner break and Linda could see at once that she was excited about something. Instead of settling down to routine work she watched as Joan methodically cleared out her desk, throwing away any rubbish.

They made their way to the canteen together and each armed herself with a tray of food before finding a table for two in a corner on their own.

"Come on, tell me what you are so excited about," Linda urged her friend as soon as they sat down. "You look ready to burst!"

"I feel it," Joan replied with a happy laugh. "You'll never guess! I'm to be assistant secretary to Mr Stapleton junior over in the other building! Isn't it exciting?"

"Oh, well done, I am glad," Linda congratulated her, but then her face fell. "Crumbs! It will be awful without you," she added with feeling.

"Don't be silly. You are doing fine," Joan told her. "Before you know where you are, you will be moving up yourself."

"Some hope. Tessa is senior to me and so are all the others, if it comes to that. Phew! It's going to be ghastly if Tessa takes your place as Miss Cornell's right-hand man."

"Miss Cornell is no fool," Joan said thoughtfully. "She knows more about Tessa and the rest of us than you think. You mark my words, she will turn more and more to you if you continue as you are at present, honest and trustworthy and ready to put your back into your work."

Linda was silent for a minute.

"What's on your mind to-day?" her friend asked her, and the story of Tessa and the telephone call came out.

"I've been wondering ever since what I should have done about it," she confessed.

"There was very little you could do," her friend assured her. "I'm afraid there is all too much lying when someone attempts to save herself from any extra effort. And it wouldn't have done for you to have a full-tilt row, either. No man wants his office full of bickering females! As a junior, the most you can do is set a good example of absolute honesty and then, when you are promoted, you can do more to stamp it out."

"I suppose you're right," Linda agreed.

"Let's change the subject or we will both have in-digestion," Joan said suddenly. "Did you enjoy yourself on Saturday? Or were we all terribly stodgy?"

Linda laughed.

"I loved it," she admitted. "Mind you, I'm still a bit

baffled about the talk at the end, but there was nothing that put me off."

"What was it that 'baffled' you then?" Joan asked.

"Oh, just the last bit. I thought we were all automatically Christians because we aren't Mohammedans or Hindus or anything like that. After all, we live in a Christian country, don't we?"

"So-called, yes. But listen," her friend argued. "If an African and his wife came to live in England, would you say that their children would be white and English children?"

"Of course not! The children would be the same as their parents."

"But people of any race can be Christians so surely the fact that you and I are English has nothing to do with it?"

"I suppose not," Linda agreed slowly. "Then how do we become Christians? I don't want to turn all religious."

"Nor do I," Joan agreed with a smile. "The Bible doesn't tell us to turn religious, either. If you read your Bible right through you would find no verses like this: He that goes to church shall become a Christian. Or, He that gives money to the missionaries and lives a good life shall become a Christian. Or even, He that reads his Bible and says his prayers shall become a Christian."

"Well, what does it say, then," Linda asked in bewilderment. "I thought all those things were good."

"So they are, but they come after a person is a Christian. The Bible says, 'He that hath the Son hath life; and he that hath not the Son of God hath not life.' That is very clear. Then in another place it says, 'Believe on the Lord Jesus Christ, and thou shalt be saved.' "

"Saved from what?" Linda butted in.

"From the punishment we deserve for our sinful lives. God is a God of righteousness and sin must be punished, but, in His Love, He sent His Son, Jesus Christ to be punished for us when He died on the cross. When we realise that in our heart of hearts, it makes us terribly sorry that we are so sinful and we want to spend the rest of our lives living for him."

"I've never heard anything like that," Linda admitted. "It all sounds wonderful." She paused and then went on, "Do you think I could join in with you and your friends and learn more about it?"

"Do. We'd love you to. And please talk to Mrs Chandler or myself if you think we can help you to understand."

"I will," Linda promised and they finished their meal and made their way back to their work.

When five o'clock came, Linda had only two of the order forms left to type and so decided to stay on and finish them. They did not take her long and she was just putting her things away in the deserted office when the door opened and Mr Stapleton came in.

"Oh dear. Are you alone?" he greeted her as she rose to her feet.

"Yes, sir. The others left a quarter of an hour ago."

"So I see," Mr Stapleton agreed, looking at his watch. "What a nuisance. I have been kept at a Board Meeting and have an important letter I wanted to send out to-night." He made his way to the door, but Linda sprang after him.

"Perhaps I could take it for you, sir," she offered, her face flushed and eager.

He looked at her and laughed gently.

"There's no harm in trying, is there? Come through to my office and we will see what we can do."

Picking up a pad and pencil, Linda followed him through and took her place in the secretary's chair beside his desk.

At first, through sheer nerves, she felt as if she had forgotten all her shorthand and missed an important figure near the beginning. She daren't stop so went right on to the end, gradually forgetting the excitement and taking the words with ease.

"Now read it back," Mr Stapleton said suddenly and Linda plucked up courage to ask him the missing figure before reading it all through.

"Well done," he greeted her effort and sent her off to transcribe her work into a proper letter.

"I shall be busy in here so will sign the letter when it is ready," he told her.

Linda headed the paper with great care, her fingers feeling stiff with anxiety, but at last it was finished and she pulled it out of the typewriter and looked at it. "Letters are a firm's ambassadors," she murmured to herself and knocked timidly on the Head Office door.

"All finished?" Mr Stapleton greeted her in a fatherly manner and then sent her away bursting with pride by adding, "I don't know what I should have done without you."

Addressing the envelope with great care Linda slipped the letter in her jacket pocket with three pennies of her own, as the stamps were locked away in Miss Cornell's office and the Post Room was shut.

The bus came on time and Linda smiled at her rush in the morning and all that had happened since then.

When she eventually got out again she was humming a tune merrily to herself as she made her way along the road to the Post Office near Hillside Estate.

"Hallo!" a voice greeted her unexpectedly and Richard Thomas drew up on his bicycle and stopped to speak. "You were on the picnic on Saturday, weren't you?" he asked her. "Did you like it?"

"Very much," Linda told him.

"And you are also the Post Girl at Stapletons, aren't you?" he went on. "Shall we introduce ourselves? My name is Richard Thomas."

"And mine's Linda Lewis," she told him, wondering whether to tell him that for at least one hour she had been Mr Stapleton's private secretary and not the Post Girl at all!

They talked for a few minutes and Richard warmly invited her to keep coming to the Friday Club and then Linda left him and hurried home to explain once again why she was late for supper.

When they had finished, she and her brother and sister washed up to give their mother a rest and they spent the rest of the evening ragging each other and having some fun.

It was half-past nine when Mrs Lewis made a move and began to tidy things up.

"Take your jacket up with you when you go, Linda," she said, picking it up and handing it to Linda, who took it and was suddenly rooted with horror.

The letter!

She had forgotten to post it.

With talking to Richard it had slipped from her mind. Whatever should she do?

"Is something the matter, dear?" her mother asked her. "You look as if you have seen a ghost."

"I never posted the letter," Linda said faintly, drawing it out of her pocket and looking at it.

"It will do in the morning," her mother tried to comfort her.

"That's just the point, it won't do in the morning. It must go to-night." She slipped on her jacket and made for the door.

"Where are you going?" her father called after her.

"To the General Post Office," Linda shouted back and raced out of the house and fetched her bicycle.

What a thing to do, she thought to herself. And the very first time she had been entrusted with something special.

It was dark when she reached the Post Office and she fumbled with the pennies in the slot machine.

Had she caught the post? She strained her eyes to see, but the little slot, which should have told her the time of the next post, was empty, and she had to be content that the letter had gone and hope it would reach its destination the following day.

# CHAPTER EIGHT

Linda felt quite sick with anxiety when she entered the office next morning. Suppose Mr Stapleton expected a 'phone call first thing in reply to that letter? Or suppose he himself rang to confirm what he had said? Poor Linda! She tried to convince herself that nothing more could be done and settle down to her work, but she did not find it easy.

When lunch-time came she almost ran to the canteen and waited impatiently until Joan joined her.

"Joan, I've done a terrible thing," she blurted out at once. "I've been so upset all morning I haven't done half as much as usual."

"But surely it can't be as bad as all that?" her friend commented. "Have you lost something or mislaid a paper in the files? Do please tell me and see if I can help."

"There's nothing anyone can do," Linda said mournfully and told Joan all about the letter.

"You are a chump!" was all the comfort she received when she had told her friend everything. "Didn't you know that there are posts every hour or so from the General? And, anyway, if you had not been here last night the letter wouldn't even have been written until this morning."

"I suppose you are right," Linda agreed. "But I was so

upset with myself after Mr Stapleton had allowed me to do it."

"Having cheered you up I shall now tick you off," Joan said with mock severity. "First and foremost, that letter should never have been tucked away in your jacket pocket. And secondly, I'm sure you know as well as I do that a secretary must never let her private worries or unhappiness interfere with her work."

"You are right as usual," Linda agreed once more. "But how one is meant to learn such self-control, I don't know."

"By practice. If you want to stay at the bottom of any job then do it half-heartedly. If you want to rise to the top then put your whole heart in it."

Joan paused and then laughed.

"If you ask me, our meals are becoming lectures. You'll be changing your meal-time to miss me soon!"

"No fear," Linda replied. "I've always wanted to make a success of my life and you seem to have the know-how that I need."

During the afternoon Linda learned even more about self-control, because she went back ready to work with a will and Tessa, who disliked anyone to show enthusiasm, did all she could to upset her.

At last, she could stand it no longer and was about to complain when the door opened and Mr Stapleton came in, looking flushed and angry. He made his way straight to Miss Cornell and Linda's heart sank. Perhaps, after all that Joan had said, there was going to be trouble about the letter.

The atmosphere in the room was electric. Each girl

typed furiously as if they knew that trouble was in the offing and, even above the noise of the machines, Mr Stapleton's voice could be heard, although it was not possible to hear what he said.

"Stop your work, girls," Miss Cornell said suddenly, and a hush fell on the room while Mr Stapleton swung on his heel and left them.

"I wish to know where each one of you was at nine-thirty yesterday morning."

One by one they told her and a handful admitted they had been in the office.

"Now which of you answered the telephone at exactly half-past nine?" she continued.

As no one replied, Miss Cornell asked each of them in turn, coming to Tessa last.

"Then it was you, Tessa, was it?" she thundered. "Let me tell you that a very good client of ours was asked by Mr Stapleton to ring up at that time. He was at London Airport on his way through to the States and when he rang he was told that Mr Stapleton was not in. He has written a card expressing his surprise and displeasure and putting Mr Stapleton in a very embarrassing position. Don't you realise that when you are on the 'phone you are the mouthpiece of the firm?"

Tessa rose to her feet and glared at Miss Cornell.

"How was I to know who it was?" she asked rudely.

But Miss Cornell was too angry to speak to her there and swept her out of the room to continue in the passage outside.

Linda swallowed to relieve the tension in her throat. It

E

was an easy thing to do if you thought the caller would ring again, but what a mess it had put everyone in.

When at last, Tessa reappeared, she flounced into the room, grabbed her personal things and rushed out again, muttering to herself that she had never liked the job anyway and was not staying any longer.

That was the last they saw of Tessa.

For a while the room was tense and uneasy and the girls said very little, but before it was time for them to go they were all back to normal and working well to make up in some way for the trouble over the 'phone call.

On her way home that evening, Linda thought about Tessa and felt sorry for her. Perhaps it was just her nature or her upbringing or pure selfishness, but Tessa had never put her back into her work and had begrudged anyone else doing so.

Walking along thinking of all that had happened, she suddenly saw Peter Johnson gazing in a radio-shop window and went across to talk to him.

"Hello, Pete," she began. "How's life?"

"Not bad," he muttered and scarcely glanced at her.

"Is something wrong?" she went on and he looked at her straight in the eye.

"It didn't take you long to find company to your taste, did it?" he said darkly.

"I don't understand," Linda replied, obviously puzzled.

"Oh, come off it! Of course you understand," Peter argued. "I saw you on Saturday. I had to go down town for a tin of paint and I saw you with all those others outside the chapel."

"Well, what of it?" Linda asked, her temper rising.

"What's wrong with going on a picnic with a friend from work?"

"So you admit it, then?" Peter growled.

"Admit what?" Linda retorted angrily.

"You must think I'm dim," Peter replied sullenly. "I saw you and I saw you last night, and each time you were with Richard Thomas!"

Linda watched him, dumbfounded, as he leapt on his motor bike and sped away.

# CHAPTER NINE

THE weeks came and went and turned into months until, a year after joining the firm, Linda found herself to be one of the senior girls in the General Office, at the beck and call of Miss Cornell.

Joan had another step up quite quickly and became assistant to Miss Cornell in Mr Stapleton's office.

Linda often wondered why Miss Cornell remained in charge of them while doing Mr Stapleton's work as well, and one day Joan told her.

"She's very efficient, you know," Joan assured her.

"I know, that's why I often wonder why she stays in charge of us instead of giving her full time to Mr Stapleton."

"I can satisfy your curiosity for you on that point," her friend told her and Linda looked up with interest.

"Until a couple of years ago the firm was quite small and Miss Cornell kept an eye on the few girls who were gradually added as orders increased. Then young Mr Stapleton came down from Oxford and joined his father and put a new zeal in the place. He is young and enthusiastic and full of ideas. I believe his father opposed his ideas for a while, but then he let him go ahead and, well, now we can hardly cope with all the orders."

"And Miss Cornell was stuck with two jobs. Surely

she could have left the General Office and stayed with
Mr Stapleton?"

"It isn't as easy as all that. You see she looks after a
crippled father, which means she cannot leave home even
for a night, and that might be awkward."

"But Mr Stapleton never goes anywhere."

"He hasn't up to now, anyway," Joan replied rather
mysteriously, and would not be drawn out any more.

But Joan was not tied in the same way as Miss Cornell
and she had not been in the Head Office long before she
disappeared for three days telling Linda she was "on
business", but keeping the type of business secret.

"You would have thought she would have told me
where she was going," she grumbled at tea that evening.

"Perhaps she isn't allowed to," her brother suggested.

"But I shouldn't tell anyone if she told me not to."

"If a thing is secret, it is secret," her father joined in.
"I remember in the war we were all told to keep quiet in
case we said anything that might help the enemy. They
used to put up great big placards, 'Be like Dad . . . Keep
Mum.' Do you remember them, dear?" he said, turning
to his wife.

"I certainly do. And I remember you came to me
one night and said goodbye because you were going away,
and it wasn't until quite a bit later that I knew you had
taken part in the invasion of Europe. You never said a
word."

"That's just the point. It may not seem so important
now, but if Joan has been told to say nothing then she is
only doing her job properly if she keeps quiet, even when
she is with her best friend."

"Ah well," George said with mock solemnity, "all we have to keep secret now is Linda's new boy friend!"

He ducked as Linda flung a cushion at him and it hit the radio sending it right to the edge of its table.

"Hey, steady on," their father told them, making a grab at the radio and restoring it to its rightful place. "There's no need to be quite so touchy!"

"He's awfully nice, anyway," Mary observed innocently.

"Who is, dear?" her mother asked.

"Linda's new friend, Richard Thomas," Mary went on.

Linda stood in the middle of the room and stamped her foot.

"Will you all stop being so stupid?" she almost shouted at them and she looked so angry that they all fell quiet and got on with their various occupations.

At last, when the silence had gone on some time, Linda began to laugh.

"I'm sorry," she said, "but you look so funny!"

They all laughed with her at that and then her father changed the subject.

"Tell me what you have been doing all this time at that factory of yours, Linda," he asked her. "You never bring home any samples of their chocolates."

"I'm afraid I see very little of that side," Linda said ruefully. "When I first started I was taken all round and watched the cocoa beans come in and the oil being extracted and each process down to the finished article. It was fascinating to watch the different centres being coated with chocolate and then all moving along a conveyor belt to be put in boxes."

"Didn't they let you eat any?" Mary asked eagerly.

"Yes, they did that day. But not now! I was treated as a visitor then; now I am part of the job, so I just have to tell other people how good the chocolates are and try to increase trade."

"Well, if you are not eating chocolates all day, what are you doing?" her father asked her.

Linda settled herself on the settee beside him.

"O.K.," she said. "I will tell you just what I have done all day to-day," and she began to describe her usual job with the post and the various typing tasks she had done.

"Then, about mid-morning there was a flap over a missing letter which had been wrongly filed and I was asked to try to find it. Honestly, it was as good as lost! There wasn't a sign of it in its right place or anywhere near it, so I had to set to and go through all the files."

"How do you 'file' things, as you call it?" Mary asked with interest.

"Well," Linda began. "Everything had been lumped together under departments since the days when there was not much business. It was chaos. Masses and masses of stuff about all different things in the same file."

"So what did our perfect secretary do about that?" George enquired.

"I was a bit scared to touch anything on my own," Linda admitted. "Then Miss Cornell came over and asked me if I could help her to sort things out a bit and we spent the entire afternoon at the job.

"We took one department at a time and divided the letters and things into subject divisions and gave each department a different coloured folder. For instance, Sales Department now has a different file for each country but all the files are blue. Then on the front of each file we put a typed list of the subjects included and the whole thing has a card index and cross-reference system to help in finding things at a moment's notice."

Linda stopped and smiled at them all.

"Sorry to get so carried away by it all," she apologised, "but I do love the work."

"I'd rather you than me!" George admitted and laughed. "I'd be the one to change colours like a chameleon if I started on a job like that!"

"Me, too," Mary agreed, while their mother picked up her knitting and then gave them all a good laugh by remarking quietly:

"Well, I'm glad you like your work, dear, but it doesn't mean a thing to me. I thought a file was for doing your nails or rubbing down a piece of wood!"

"Really, Mother!" Linda gasped in the burst of laughter that followed.

It was a couple of days later that Linda had another opportunity to prove herself.

Miss Cornell was in Mr Stapleton's office taking some letters when the internal telephone rang and Linda found herself speaking to Mr Stapleton junior.

"Can someone come and take some letters for me?" he said. "I have had to send Miss Mathews home with a headache."

"Certainly, sir," Linda replied immediately and put down the 'phone.

"If Miss Cornell wants to know where I am, tell her I

am with young Mr S., will you?" she said, turning to one of the others.

With her pad and pencil in her hand she hurried down the passage hoping she was doing right. It reminded her of that other evening when she took her first letter a year before and then forgot to post it!

There were three letters to take and she managed quite well, except when the flow was broken and something added as an afterthought. When, eventually, she transcribed them, on two occasions she spoiled her letter and had to begin again because she came across an insertion later on.

"What is this work?" Miss Cornell asked her, coming up without Linda noticing, and Linda explained what had happened and how she had taken the letters herself.

"I do hope I didn't do wrong," she added anxiously.

"Wrong? Certainly not. I am very glad you used your initiative and intelligence," Miss Cornell praised her. "When you have finished the letters, you may take them in for signature yourself and ask Mr Stapleton if there is anything else you can do for him."

"Thank you, Miss Cornell, I will," Linda replied happily.

But when, eventually, she took the letters through, the office was empty and she had to be content to leave them on the desk to await a signature.

# CHAPTER TEN

ONE morning, near the end of November, Linda woke up and lay listening and the world outside sounded strangely muffled. She climbed out of bed and drew back her curtains. There was dense fog! Fog so thick she couldn't even see the rose tree in the middle of their little lawn, and the gate was swallowed up in a thick, wet blanket.

"You'd better get up, Mary," she called to her sister. "It's a real pea-souper outside and I guess we shall all be late to-day."

Mary swung out of bed sleepily and joined her at the window.

"Crumbs! It's awful," she commented and gazed out for a minute before shutting the curtains again and switching on the bedroom light.

It was early and the rest of the family grumbled as the two girls woke them.

"Wassa matter?" their father gasped when they reached him.

"Fog," Linda said briefly.

"But it's only quarter to seven," her father objected.

"I know it is," Linda agreed. "But it's a very thick fog and we shall all be late."

They dressed and Linda did her hair as Mary read her Bible and spent a few moments in prayer.

"Don't you ever get sick of doing that?" Linda asked,

putting her head round her sister's door, as Mary rose from her knees.

"Sick of it? I should think not," Mary replied. "I read just a few verses and try to remember them through the day and then I thank God for a good night and tell Him what lies ahead for the day."

"Do you think He is really interested?" Linda asked thoughtfully.

"I know He is. Dad is interested when I speak to him and God is interested in what I say because He is my Heavenly Father and I am His child."

"It must be nice to be so sure about God," Linda said quietly. "I must say I am quite impressed that you have kept it up for so long."

Mary's face lit up.

"But it isn't something I just add to my life," she said. "It is a way of living—a life in itself and my Quiet Time in the morning is like a spiritual breakfast. If I miss it I feel out of sorts all day."

Linda looked at her thoughtfully and then went downstairs for her breakfast with the others.

It was a terrible day. Mr Lewis set off with the three children and they made their way to the bus stop only to find a crowd of shivering people waiting for a bus which never came.

After a while they decided to walk and started off together. At first they laughed as unexpected hazards loomed up in front of them and especially when George apologised politely to a lamp-post he brushed. Then while they were laughing, Linda trod down an unseen kerb and nearly fell.

But George soon left them to go along to the garage where he worked and not long after that their father came to the bottom of his road, too.

"Are you two sure you will be all right?" he asked the two girls.

"We'll manage, thank you, Dad," Linda told him. "I will go right along to the Grammar School with Mary and then continue on the lower road to the factory. 'Bye! Take care."

Linda and Mary went slowly on with their eyes and throats stinging and their hair wet with moisture. On and on they went until they were forced to cross the main road.

"Look out!" Linda shouted suddenly as they started to cross and a car appeared and passed only a few feet away from them, its lights probing ineffectively into the gloom ahead.

"Whew! This is beastly," Mary admitted, and they clung to each other and tried again.

Reaching the school Linda set off on her own.

It certainly was beastly. She ran her hand along the wall for guidance and tried hard not to be afraid. At one time a flood of panic filled her as she lost her bearings but she quelled the fear and, walking gingerly forward, found she was at a minor crossing she could only vaguely remember.

At last, to her great relief, she reached the factory gates and entered. It was strangely quiet and she wondered how many other stumbling figures were hidden in the fog.

The office was deserted and she switched on the lights. No Miss Cornell and none of the girls, just Linda on her

own! She looked around and draped her things over a
chair by a radiator. It was ten minutes past nine. Even
she was late in spite of her early start.

Hurrying down to the Post Room she saw one or two
others looking rather lost, as if the key to the daily activity
had been mislaid and no one could start things moving.

Down in the Post Room it was the same. No post had
arrived and one girl was sitting with her shoes off and her
feet on a radiator trying to warm herself.

Returning to the General Office Linda began to think.
Suppose Miss Cornell could not get in? And Joan, she
lived a good way away. What ought she to do?

She soon made up her mind and set to work. She,
Linda, would do all the routine morning jobs she had seen
Miss Cornell do.

She sharpened Mr Stapleton's pencils and put out clean
blotting paper and paper clips and a note pad with a clean
sheet on top. Then she turned the calendar and opened
his engagement diary at the right place. After that she
hurried to young Mr Stapleton's office and did the same
and had just returned to the General Office when the
'phone rang.

It was one of the girls. She had come so far and then
turned back and was ringing to say she would try again
later if the fog cleared.

Linda replaced the 'phone and put a note on Miss
Cornell's desk about the message. As she did so she heard
a door open and Mr Stapleton and his son walked down
the passage.

"Good morning, Miss Lewis," they greeted her when
they saw her.

"Good morning," she replied and was relieved to see two more girls from the General Office come in.

But there was no sign of either Miss Cornell or Joan. There was nothing for it but for her to carry on.

She tapped nervously on Mr Stapleton's door and entered.

"Would you tell Miss Fraser I am in?" he began and Linda had to tell him Joan had not arrived.

"It's a shocking morning. What about Miss Cornell?"

"She is not in either," Linda told him.

"Then who prepared my desk for me?" he asked.

"I did, sir. Is everything there? The post has not arrived yet," Linda informed him.

Mr Stapleton looked at her.

"You seem to be a sensible young lady," he observed slowly. "I seem to remember you helped me out of a difficulty once before, with a letter."

Linda waited, wondering what he was going to say.

"I was telling Miss Cornell only yesterday that I need someone to help Miss Fraser," he went on slowly. "She mentioned you and we were a bit bothered about your age. You are only eighteen, I believe?"

"Yes, sir," Linda breathed.

"But still," he said, throwing himself back in his chair, "it isn't age that matters so much as efficiency. How would you like to assist Miss Fraser?"

"I should like to very much," Linda gasped, trying not to look as excited as she felt.

"Then I had better give you some idea of what we are planning at the moment," Mr Stapleton went on. "I

# CHAPTER ELEVEN

IT was exciting working for Mr Stapleton. Of course Linda was not given any of his personal work, her job was to assist Joan and she was kept busy with filing and filling in sickness and leave figures and taking down draft agendas for the business meetings which seemed to crop up more and more frequently.

Now, when anything was decided, Linda knew all about it from the start and learned the art of keeping quiet when necessary on any particular subject.

She was also put in charge of distributing any stationary ordered by the other offices and kept strict details of everything sent out in a special little note-book.

"Have you seen Mr Stapleton's engagement diary?" Joan asked her anxiously one morning. "I can't find it anywhere and he will be here in a minute and wanting to go through the plans for the day with me."

"No, I haven't seen it this morning," Linda replied. "It was on his desk last night. Are you sure it isn't in any of his drawers?"

"I've been through them all and can't find it."

Just then the 'phone rang and Joan picked it up.

"Mr Stapleton's secretary speaking," she began. "Oh, yes. Good morning. Mr Bulmer would like to talk over some business with Mr Stapleton? Lunch? Yes, I think that will be all right. At the Royal at one o'clock." She gave a frantic look at Linda but her voice remained calm. "Mr Stapleton has been delayed this morning," she continued, "but if there is any reason why he cannot come I will ring you as soon as he comes in."

There was a pause.

"Infield 48. Extension 1. Thank you, goodbye."

She put the 'phone down and breathed a sigh of relief.

"Can't you find that diary anywhere?" she asked. "I know Mr Stapleton is out for lunch one day this week and I only hope it isn't to-day. That diary is an awful nuisance."

"I think I could make something more convenient if you would let me," Linda said thoughtfully.

"Well, please do," Joan replied in a worried voice and began to go through the drawers again.

A few minutes later Mr Stapleton came in and sat down at his desk. He carried a bundle of papers in his hand and on top of them was the engagement diary Joan had been wanting so much.

She picked it up with an accusing look in her eye.

"I thought this was lost, Mr Stapleton," was all she said, and breathed a sigh of relief to find there was nothing booked for lunch-time that day.

The next hour was spent in going through the engagements of the day and making sure that all necessary papers were to hand, followed by the daily task of dealing with the post. Linda took no part in either of these things so she sat down and gave a few minutes' thought to her new idea.

By the time Mr Stapleton and Joan were finished it was

all ready and she carried a small box across to them rather shyly.

"Is this your new idea for an engagement diary?" Joan asked. "May we have a look?"

Linda handed it over. Into the box she had inserted cards headed "Monday" to "Saturday" and behind each card was an ordinary ruled card such as they used in indexing.

"I thought perhaps this could stay on Joan's desk and, as an engagement was made, it could be written down on the card for that day together with any information required or a note of papers needed for the meeting or whatever it was."

"That sounds a very good idea," Mr Stapleton commented, picking up the box. "I suppose I could scribble things down, too?"

"Oh, yes, of course, sir," Linda agreed, flushing with pleasure. "It would really be better on your desk for you to see, but I thought you might not like the idea."

"We will certainly give it a try," Mr Stapleton agreed. "But now we must get down to work. Our big meeting at Prices is due to take place over the last week-end of November. Do you both think you will be able to come?"

Linda's eyes shone.

"We should have to go down first thing in the morning of Thursday of next week and return the following Tuesday afternoon. Could you manage that?"

"It will be quite all right for me," Joan assured him and they both turned to Linda.

"I expect it will be for me, too. I could let you know to-morrow for certain if that would be soon enough."

"Quite soon enough," Mr Stapleton said with a smile. "It is rather a long spell, but there is a great deal for us to do and the Director down there is anxious that I should stay the weekend to get to know his wife and family socially. We will work until midday on the Saturday and start again first thing Monday, so I think it would be hardly worth your while to travel home and back all that way."

The following Wednesday week Linda packed her things in a bright new suitcase and put on a new hat and coat which she had bought for the journey out of her savings.

"You look lovely," Mary told her as she tucked a stray wisp of hair up under her hat. "It must be ever so exciting to be so important."

Linda said nothing but her thoughts ran riot. Whatever was happening? She, Linda Lewis, who had always envied her sister her place in the Grammar School and the prizes she won so easily, she was being told she was important!

"Don't you believe it!" she said to Mary, determined not to let the remark go to her head. "I'm only going to help Joan. I'm not Mr Stapleton's secretary."

"But you're the next best thing, isn't she, Mum?" Mary said loyally.

"She's doing very well," their mother said proudly and then added, "but she'll do a lot better if she catches the train."

"Ooh, my word! Is that the time?" Linda gasped, glancing at the clock and she hurriedly gathered up her things and set off.

Arriving at the station she found Joan already there and a few minutes later both Mr Stapleton and his son joined them. Joan had booked seats and bought the tickets earlier and now had a porter all ready to take their luggage and show them into their seats. She had called at the office too and picked up the morning post, and when the train started they spent some time working on the morning's letters.

Once that was out of the way they discussed their plans for the next few days and then settled down to enjoy the rest of the journey.

For Linda it passed all too quickly and she could not understand how the others could hide themselves away behind magazines and take no notice of the lovely scenery through which they were passing.

When, eventually, they arrived and booked in at their hotel it was Joan who had seen to everything and knew just what to do. Linda watched her with admiration and wondered whether she would ever be as efficient and confident as her friend.

At last they were in their bedroom and Joan flung herself down on a chair.

"Here we are," she said. "And it may be for work but I'm sure we are going to enjoy ourselves."

"So am I," Linda agreed enthusiastically. "I have never stayed in a hotel like this before," she confided.

"Ah, well, you'll soon get used to it," Joan replied. "A good secretary must be able to cope with strange hotels and travelling arrangements, so you have an opportunity to learn."

They changed and had a good wash to refresh themselves before going down to the dining-room for lunch.

"I've been on the 'phone to Mr Bulmer," Mr Stapleton told them as they joined him. "He would like us to take a taxi out to the factory after lunch and have a good look round before we get down to work in earnest in the morning."

They found the visit to the factory very interesting. It was similar to the one they were used to but rather older, and it also had a section where boiled sweets were made. Linda gazed into the great cauldrons of boiling, sticky mixture and sniffed the pungent steam rising from them.

But there were no samples this time and she and Joan had to keep their minds on what they were doing in case they were asked for any particulars later on.

It was dark when their tour of inspection came to an end and the wind was beginning to rise. They drew their coats around them as they made their way to the car that was to take them back to their hotel.

"It looks like a storm to-night," Mr Stapleton commented, and very soon afterwards specks of rain spattered the windscreen of the car.

By the time they reached the hotel it was blowing hard and the rain was beating down. They hurried from the car into the entrance and were glad to be inside the welcoming hall.

"I think we will be independent for the rest of the evening," Mr Stapleton told them, turning to his son.

"Everything is ready for the morning and I am going to give myself the luxury of a meal in my room and an early night."

"It certainly isn't very inviting outside," his son remarked, taking off his raincoat and giving it a shake. "I think I will follow your example."

Mr Stapleton turned to the two girls.

"I shouldn't be too late either, if I were you," he advised them. "If you could make a few notes on what we saw this afternoon, then I should turn in and get a good night's sleep."

They parted and the girls took the lift to their room on the fourth floor.

"Isn't it all exciting?" Linda burst out as soon as they were alone. "Just fancy being right away from home like this and treated as if we were really grown up."

Joan laughed at her friend.

"You don't expect Mr Stapleton to read you a bed-time story, do you?" she teased her. "By the way, hadn't you better send a card home to tell your parents we have arrived safely?"

They each wrote a card and posted it in the hotel post box before having a meal in the dining-room.

By the time they went to bed the wind was whistling round and blowing great gusts, and they had to shut their window to keep out the pouring rain.

Linda watched with interest as her friend took out a Bible and read and knelt in prayer while she busied herself with face creams and curlers and touched up her nail varnish.

# CHAPTER TWELVE

I<small>T</small> was the early hours of the morning when Linda roused again and listened to the howling of the wind outside. Gradually she became aware of another noise, a steady drip, drip, drip which went on and on and on.

At first she thought it was in the room and raised herself up on her elbow to listen. Then she climbed out of bed and eased the curtain aside to allow her to see a little more. Down below the cars were still weaving their way homeward on the rain-sodden streets.

She turned back into the room to continue her search for the monotonous dripping and just then Joan woke up.

"Whatever are you doing?" she asked in a puzzled voice. "You'll be frozen. Get into bed and go to sleep."

"There's some water dripping somewhere?" Linda told her and Joan giggled sleepily.

"It's raining," she said. "Hadn't you noticed?"

Linda switched on the light and put on her dressing-gown and slippers.

"Don't be silly," she said shortly. "It's a jolly wet sort of drip and I thought it was in the room."

Once the light was on she soon found the cause of the trouble. Their room was at the end of a passage with a bathroom next door and an investigation showed that the rain had found a very substantial leak and was dripping merrily into an ever-widening pool by the bathroom door.

As Linda said later, it seemed a pity to soak a good carpet, so she took a bucket she found in the bathroom and placed it under the leak and returned to bed to the accompaniment of an even louder drip!

Back in bed she felt wide awake and was pleased to see that Joan had not gone back to sleep either.

"Do you mind if we talk?" Linda asked.

"Of course not. What shall we talk about?" her friend replied.

Linda paused for a minute.

"I don't know quite how to put it," she said. "But you and Mary and the others at the Friday Club all have something that I haven't and I want to know what it is. Mary used to be a catty little thing that put my back up before she went to the Club. Then she became quieter and quite suddenly changed. I used to tease the poor kid at first and ask her why she had turned all holy, but she didn't give up."

"And what about me?" Joan asked, encouraging her to talk.

"Well, you are similar. You both read your Bibles, which I'm sure I should find deadly dull, and you both . . . well, you're both so consistent. I mean, you aren't like some people who turn all Christian on Sundays and for the rest of the week are exactly the same as the rest of us. You sort of 'live' this Christianity business, if you see what I mean."

"I do see what you mean," Joan replied quietly. "And you are absolutely right, we do live our Christianity, or try to, from the moment we become Christians onwards."

"Could you tell me more about it?" Linda asked eagerly, and they both sat up in bed and put their dressing-gowns round their shoulders.

"O.K.," she agreed and picked up her Bible. "Let's start right at the beginning and see what it is all about. The first thing we are told is that man was created by God in His Image and man was sinless. Do you remember?"

"Yes. And then Eve was tempted to eat of the forbidden fruit and she did it and so did her husband, Adam."

"That's right. Well, the Bible tells us that everyone born into the world since that time is a sinner. Romans 3, verse 23, says, 'For all have sinned and come short of the glory of God'. Do you agree with that?"

"Yes, I suppose I do," Linda replied slowly. "It's very easy to think of sinners as murderers and drunkards and so on, but I suppose in some degree we have all sinned."

"I think we have all sinned pretty badly in one way or another," Joan replied. "Things like dishonesty and envy and bad temper and bitterness and lying and so on are all sins when you come to think of them."

"Then I'm in it with the rest of you pretty badly," Linda agreed solemnly. "Where do we go from there?"

"The next step is even worse. Once we realise that every one of us is a sinner, we try to find a way out by good works and struggling to do better, only to find that the Bible says again in Romans but this time chapter 6, verse 23, 'The wages of sin is death'."

"Why 'wages'?" Linda broke in.

"Because wages are what you earn by what you do and death is what you earn by being a sinner."

"But I'm not dead and yet we've just agreed that I'm a sinner."

"It doesn't mean physical death as we talk of death," Joan explained, "but separation from God spiritually, not only now but in the life to come."

They were quiet for a moment and the noise of the wind filled the room. Then Linda said in a puzzled voice:

"You've got me scared, Joan. First you convince me I'm a sinner, then you say I can't do anything about it, and, finally, you tell me that God's punishment for sin is death. It's awful!"

"You're right, it is awful," Joan agreed. "At least it would be if that was the end of the story, but it isn't. God still loves us. There is still another verse I want to read to you from Romans, this time chapter 5, verse 8. It reads, 'But God commendeth His love towards us, in that, while we were yet sinners, Christ died for us.' God didn't write us off, Linda. He thought of a way in which He could be absolutely just in his punishment for sin and yet still make it possible for us to be with Him some day."

"What did He do?" Linda asked eagerly.

"He sent His Son, Jesus Christ, to the earth to die in our place. He was the only person ever to be free from sin and He allowed men to take Him and crucify Him on the cross at Calvary in your place and mine."

"You say Christ died in my place and took my punishment?" Linda said in an awed voice. "But that is wonderful. Whatever can I do to thank Him?"

"Just tell Him so," Joan explained. "Let's get on our knees now and tell Him how sorry you are you ever sinned and made it necessary for Him to die for you—if you are sorry."

"Oh, I am," Linda muttered with a catch in her voice. "To think that the beastly part of me caused the Son of God to die."

She got out of bed and sank on her knees with her friend by her side and when she stood up again there was a new joy in her face Joan had never seen before.

The following day was long and busy and the girls had slept little, but there was a joy which they shared that carried them through as they attended endless meetings and discussions and took down many headings and summaries.

Saturday afternoon came at last and the two girls breathed a sigh of relief as they were free to go out for a while before catching up with their notes.

"Let's take a bus and get away from the crowds and have a good walk in the country," Joan suggested.

"That would be rather fun," Linda agreed. "If we stay around here we are sure to be tempted to spend a lot of money in some of the big shops."

So they caught a bus and, by half-past two, were striding along in the open country.

"Everything looks different, here," Linda commented. "I suppose it is just because I don't know it! It is so easy to take beauty for granted when you see it every day."

"I know what you mean," Joan agreed. "Down by the river at home isn't a bit exciting because we can always go there. I suppose it's as lovely to us here as other people must find the old Thames at home."

"Very clearly put, I don't think!" Linda said with a laugh and they turned off the road to follow a footpath running beside a little stream.

They walked on together in silence for a while enjoying the colours in the heather and bracken and the crystal clear water bustling along over the pebbles beside them.

"I think I should be happier than I have ever been if it were not for one thing," Linda said suddenly.

"Oh?" Joan replied, stopping and looking at her friend. "Can I help or do you want to keep it to yourself?"

Linda kicked a stone and watched it bounce off a boulder into the stream before she replied.

"The snag is, I know what you will say," she admitted. "But I think I should feel better if I gave the subject an airing—if you don't mind?" she said with a sigh.

"Go on," Joan said quietly, stooping to pick up a handful of pebbles and drop them one by one into the water.

"It's like this," Linda began. "I've never told you, but, ever since I was tiny, I have been friendly with a boy at home called Peter Johnson. Pete and I sort of clicked, if you see what I mean. We both like the same sort of things and are both full of ambition and, the truth is, I've always been rather fond of him."

She paused but Joan said nothing.

"Everything was O.K. until I started going out with the Friday Club folk and then he got the silly idea in his head that I was friendly with someone else and was giving him the push. I was intending to make it up with him when we got home next week, but he isn't going to like it if I tell him I have taken Christ as my Saviour. Shall I keep quiet and see if he notices the difference?"

Joan stood up and faced her friend.

"What do you think is the right thing to do?" she asked. "I should tell him. If he cuts you off then God will have something better for you. You can't start your Christian life by being ashamed to own it."

Linda smiled rather sadly.

"I knew all along you would say something like that," she admitted. "There isn't any choice, really, is there?"

They continued their walk for a little while before turning round to make their way back to catch the bus.

"We haven't left ourselves very long," Joan said, glancing at her watch. "I think we had better hurry." She set off quickly with Linda close behind.

The bus was not in sight as they drew nearer the road and Linda looked at the heather at her feet.

"You go on slowly and give me a shout when the bus is coming. I'm going to pick a tiny bunch of heather to cheer us up as we transcribe our notes," she told Joan, and she started to pick at once as Joan wandered on on her own.

She had scarcely picked anything when Joan shouted:

"Quick, Linda, there are two roads up here and the bus is coming."

Glancing up she saw Joan scrambling up the bank by the stream and running toward the bus stop.

Picking up her handbag and clutching her bunch of heather, Linda set off as fast as she could along the water's edge, running and jumping from one firm tuft to the next.

"Come on!" Joan encouraged her, taking her attention for a moment and, as she did so, Linda missed the next tuft and landed over her ankles in a patch of muddy bog. What a mess! But there was no time for cleaning up and she pulled herself clear and stumbled on, her shoes oozing and squelching with every step.

Joan had one foot on the bus and was persuading the conductor to wait when Linda reached her. One look was enough.

"Whatever in the world have you been doing?" she burst out and they almost fell into the bus with laughing.

Poor Linda. Everyone turned to see what was happening and she had to sit, still clutching the precious heather, with her feet tucked out of sight under the seat.

Reaching their hotel Linda felt sure everyone would notice the filthy state she was in and hurried to their room as fast as possible. Joan, on the other hand, followed more slowly still trying hard not to giggle.

When at last they were in the privacy of their room Linda pulled off her shoes and stockings and had a good wash at once.

"I might tell you the filthy stuff was freezing," she snorted as Joan held up a stocking and went off into fits of laughter again.

"You poor dear," she sympathised, pulling herself together. "I should keep your slippers on and get warm, if I were you. I'll wash these things for you."

"Thanks awfully," Linda said gratefully. "I'm not annoyed really," she added. "It's just that I felt such a silly chump plastered in mud like that. I'm so thankful I didn't sit in it!"

Putting a match to the gas fire they drew up a table and began to transcribe their notes ready for Monday morning.

"Never a dull moment," Linda murmured as her fingers tapped the keys and they settled down and worked hard to catch up with their work.

# CHAPTER THIRTEEN

BY the time Tuesday afternoon came even Linda was glad to be going home. She had enjoyed every minute of the trip away, but they had all been so busy from early morning until late at night that she felt worn out.

"Have you had an interesting time?" her father asked as she dumped her suitcase in the hall and pulled off her hat.

"I've had a wonderful time," Linda replied, and began to tell them everything. She was tempted to leave out the night of the storm but in the end told them quite simply what had happened that night.

"But, how wonderful!" Mary exclaimed at once, her eyes shining. "I've been praying for you for ages."

"O.K.," George grunted uncomfortably. "Let's cut that talk out, shall we? What was the hotel like, Sis.?"

Linda squeezed Mary's arm and smiled at her.

"It was terrific, George. All thick carpets and people in uniform," she answered her brother. She felt so happy that she had been able to speak up for her Lord straight away.

Back at work everything went on as before until one day Miss Cornell sent for Linda.

"This factory is growing too fast for my liking," the older woman grumbled. "I have to move people here and there and promote them before they have held a job for five minutes."

Linda wondered what it was all about.

"You seem to be developing very well, Linda," Miss Cornell said as if she had only just noticed she was not alone. "Do you think you could manage as a full secretary now?" Without waiting for Linda to reply she hurried on. "Mr Stapleton junior is going to be without a secretary very soon. Miss Mathews has got herself engaged to be married just when we thought she was settled and she says she must leave and prepare for her wedding, as her fiancé is moving out of the district and they have to find a house somewhere up in the north. It all seems rather rushed to me. But there, it's none of my business."

It was obvious that Miss Cornell was flustered and not a little annoyed, so Linda waited quietly while her heart beat fast with excitement.

"I think one of the girls from the General Office could help Miss Fraser and you could move over to young Mr Stapleton's office. What do you feel about it?"

"I should like to very much, Miss Cornell," Linda replied eagerly. "Will Miss Mathews be here long enough to show me the ropes?"

"She intends to leave at the end of the month, giving you just over a fortnight. I think that should be enough, but, let me warn you, Mr Stapleton is not like his father. He has ideas of his own and it will be up to you to learn how to do things as he likes them done, which will not necessarily be the way you do them now."

Linda felt she was walking on air as she made her way

back to her desk, but she could not tell Joan for some time, as they were all busy. When, at last, she found a free moment, Joan was as pleased as she and they raced through the afternoon's work together very happily.

Linda's mind was far away when she got out of the bus on the way home and she walked slowly along the pavement. She was wonderfully happy and decided to buy herself a bar of chocolate in celebration.

Crossing to the shop, she was about to enter when the door opened and she came face to face with Peter.

"Pete!" she exclaimed. "I haven't seen you for ages. Where have you been?"

He stood in front of her and lit a cigarette before he replied.

"I don't see that it matters to you where I have been," he replied at last, throwing the match down with a flick of his wrist.

"What has come over you, Peter?" Linda asked anxiously. "I haven't done anything to break our friendship. It's just that we haven't seen very much of each other for a long time."

Peter looked at her.

"Listen, Lindy," he said and walked her away from the shop to where they could talk privately. "We've had a lot of happy times one way and another in the past. Let's leave it like that. You have new interests and new friends and, well, so have I."

Linda stared at him.

"I have new friends at work and at the Friday Club, but I thought you were annoyed at that."

"I was a little while ago," Peter said with a laugh. "I

thought you would be coming and asking me to join you at one of your Bible Studies, and then I thought how silly I was and how much better it would be if I made my own friends. So I applied for a job away from home and have been away three weeks. That's why you haven't seen me."

"Away?" Linda echoed.

"Yes. I'm just home for a few days. I'm glad I've seen you. Now we can each go our own way and no one will be hurt."

"Peter, you're right. I would have asked you to come to the Friday Club because belief in God is the only answer to life, but you shouldn't have gone away."

"I don't understand what you see in religion," he said quietly. "And, I must admit, I don't particularly want to, so, really, it is just as well that I shall not be around."

He put out his hand and she found herself shaking it. Then, he was gone.

Linda's mind was in a turmoil as she made her way home. Peter had always been such a good friend and now he had gone out of her life and she felt very sad. She thought back to all the happy times they had spent together and then she thought of the night her life had changed and a great peace crept into her heart as she realised that God had a plan for her life and she must be willing for Him to have His way, even if it hurt.

Two weeks later Linda found herself hard at work in her new office.

"I like to dictate my letters to this dictaphone here," Mr Stapleton told her on the very first morning she was on her own. "It saves a great deal of time for me and you can then transcribe the work when you have the office to yourself. Also my handwriting is atrocious," he added with a smile.

"Would you mind showing me what I have to do?" Linda asked with interest. She had seen the dictaphone in use before she took over in the office, but had not been able to go near it.

Mr Stapleton explained the knobs to her and waited until she felt she knew all about working it before turning to some papers he had been checking about the amalgamation.

Linda, meanwhile, had a look through his private files to make quite sure she could lay her hands on anything that was needed at a moment's notice. It was vital to the smooth running of the office that there should be give and take between manager and secretary, but, if she was to help him to be efficient, she must know exactly where everything was kept.

"It all seems so different," she confided in Joan when they met at lunch.

"How do you mean?"

"I don't really know. It's tidy enough, but that's about all. I've already made a card index box for appointments; at least it will be useful to me even if no one else uses it."

"What about a note-book of names, addresses and 'phone numbers of people you are in touch with frequently?" Joan suggested.

"That's a good idea. And I must do something about incoming calls, too. At the moment I just try to remember them or scribble them on a scrap of paper."

All was quiet in the afternoon and Linda decided to try out the dictaphone and see if she could have the letters finished by the time Mr Stapleton returned from a luncheon engagement.

It was rather like a toy at first and she smiled as a deep voice recited the letters to her from the desk.

Suddenly the 'phone rang and she leaned to pick it up, pressing a knob to stop the dictaphone as she did so. It was a complaint about some chocolate and she had to take down the full details so that she was sure to report it correctly.

Putting back the 'phone Linda was surprised to find the tape on the dictaphone still revolving but she switched it back to the beginning again and began to listen. All went well until she reached the part where she had been disturbed.

Then, horrors! Nothing happened after that. She tried again and then looked at it carefully and the truth dawned. Somehow she had pressed the wrong knob and wiped out the rest of the letters she was supposed to type!

Almost sick with anxiety and very annoyed with herself for being so stupid, she waited until young Mr Stapleton returned and then told him what had happened.

For a moment she thought he was going to be very angry, but then, all of a sudden, he threw back his head and gave such a roar of laughter that she expected Miss Cornell to come rushing in to see what was going on.

From that moment they worked together as a team and Linda had only one complaint. Two or three days after she took over in the office Mr Stapleton received a 'phone call from his wife.

"Miss Lewis," he said, half apologetically, as he put down the receiver. "Would you be good enough to slip into the town for me? I'll make out a shopping list for you."

Linda's mouth opened and she was about to protest that shopping was hardly secretarial work when she decided it would probably be more dignified to cope somehow and not complain, so she put on her coat and stood waiting.

"I will put things right with my father," Mr Stapleton assured her. "My wife isn't too fit just now."

"I'm sorry about that," Linda replied rather shortly, and she hurried out with a list of things to buy and a great deal of work to do on her return.

"If this isn't about the limit," she murmured as she went.

## CHAPTER FOURTEEN

As time went by, and Linda reached and passed her twentieth birthday, she enjoyed her work more and more. She became quick and efficient and Mr Stapleton began to rely on her very much and several times she accompanied him to the new branch of the firm.

One morning, putting out everything that was needed for the day's work, she settled down to sort and file the previous day's papers. Mr Stapleton had usually arrived by the time she finished doing this, but this day he was late and she went through the post again to make sure everything necessary was ready and the files that would be needed were there.

It was half-past nine.

Opening the door she looked across to the General Office where everything appeared to be quite normal and busy. Further down the passage she could just see Joan through the glass-panelled door discussing something with the Managing Director, but there was still no sign of young Mr Stapleton and Linda began to feel a little anxious.

However, she had plenty to do and spent some time duplicating some papers which she had put into her drawer for an opportunity like this.

It was almost eleven o'clock when she covered up the duplicator and collated the papers two by two ready for stapling. By then she thought it was quite time she found out what had happened to Mr Stapleton.

Picking up her internal 'phone she rang through to Joan.

"I say, Joan," she began at once, "I don't want to alarm old Mr Stapleton but his son hasn't made an appearance this morning. Has he, by any chance, given you a hint that something might have happened?"

"Just a minute, please," Joan replied in a business-like manner. Then she heard her continue: "There is an enquiry for young Mr Stapleton, sir," she said tactfully, but Linda could not hear the reply.

"If he isn't in his office I should ring round the factory," Joan replied in a guarded voice.

"Thank you, I will," Linda answered and added quietly, "I'm getting a bit anxious. Goodbye."

It did not take long to ring the various departments but with no result. Each one told her he would be in his office and Linda did not wish to upset everyone, so rang off without saying any more.

Quite obviously he was not at work at all but Linda was loth to ring up his home, so she decided to walk round and make sure he was not busy somewhere and no one had noticed.

She looked everywhere. In a new wing they were building; down in the Post Room; at the Gate House and then again through the factory itself on her way back to the office.

"You look worried. Is anything wrong?" someone asked her as she made her way past great troughs of steaming chocolate.

"Richard!" she exclaimed with relief. "I suppose it is silly, but I'm so relieved to find someone to talk to," and she told him what the trouble was about.

"You mustn't worry, Linda," he told her. "I expect young Mr Stapleton has a perfectly good reason for being out to-day but has just forgotten to tell you."

"But he was very quiet and not at all his usual self yesterday," Linda told him. "You don't think he can have had an accident, do you?"

"Of course not. The police would have been here long ago," he assured her. He smiled down at her and went on gently. "It isn't right for Christians like you and me to get in a flap. Just tell the Lord about it and then go and ring up his home."

Linda smiled gratefully.

"Thank you, Richard. I will," she said and left him.

She had hardly taken a dozen steps when a cry rang out and she turned quickly to see Richard already hurrying across the factory to where one of the apprentices was doubled up in pain.

"What happened?" she asked, joining them and gently easing the boy's hand from where he clutched it to him.

"It was the machine," he gasped. "I was just going to put on the safety guard, honest I was."

"Poor kid," Richard commented and sat him on a bench nearby while Linda looked at the crushed fingers.

"Get me the first aid kit, please," she said and undid the boy's tie as he turned deathly pale.

Richard hurried off and returned with the kit and gave it to her.

By now the foreman had joined them and helped her

clean up the filthy hand and remove some of the grease and dirt to see how much damage had been done. Then she turned to the boy.

"What is your name?" she asked him.

"Bill Stevens," he replied.

"I'm afraid you will have to go down to the hospital, Bill, and get this patched up," she told him. Turning to Richard she went on:

"Do you think we could use the work's car?"

"I'll go and see, Miss Lewis," he replied. "He'll be all right to go on his own, won't he?"

Linda looked at the boy who, by this time, was shaking from head to foot with the shock of the accident.

"If you will keep an eye on him," she told Richard, "I will make enquiries about the car."

In the end Miss Cornell gave Linda permission to go herself with Bill, especially as Mr Stapleton had still not put in an appearance.

"I can't understand it at all," she said. "But I'll tell him where you are if he arrives and, if not, then I think you had better tell his father when you return."

As it turned out, the hospital staff were very glad that Linda had taken Bill straight down there. One of his fingers was badly crushed and there was considerable repair work for them to do, which meant he would have to go to the operating theatre.

She left him reluctantly and promised to see that his mother was told and then hurried out of the hospital towards the waiting car.

As she reached it she noticed the driver was gazing beyond her with a puzzled look on his face and, turning, who should be following her but young Mr Stapleton and looking as pleased as punch with himself.

"Mr Stapleton!" she exclaimed and waited for him to come up to her. "Are you all right? I beg your pardon, sir, but I was getting very anxious when you did not come in this morning."

"Oh, didn't I 'phone?" he replied dreamily. "I'm so sorry, I meant to." Then, with a grin like a school-boy, he looked at her. "You'll have to forgive me, you see, my wife has just presented me with a baby son!"

Linda stared at him. So that was why she had been sent out shopping. Why ever hadn't he told her?

Suddenly she came back to earth.

"I'm so glad," she said warmly. "My congratulations, sir, and may I wish the baby—your son—God's richest blessing."

She climbed into the car after him, amused that he never questioned her as to why she or the car were at the hospital at all!

Back at the factory old Mr Stapleton was overjoyed to hear of his grandson's arrival and, in a very short while, the news spread and an atmosphere of joy and celebration filled the place.

It was not until almost time to go home that Linda found herself alone with young Mr Stapleton in the office.

"I've been thinking," he said suddenly and Linda looked up from her work.

"Everyone has been congratulating me all day and talking about the third generation of Stapletons in the factory and all that sort of thing, and it has sounded very thrilling. Only you, of all the people who have spoken to me, have wished the baby 'God's richest blessing', I think that was how you put it. What did you mean by that?"

Linda flushed and sent up a quick prayer for help that she should say the right thing.

"Well," she stammered. "I don't know if you will understand. You see, most people, given the opportunity and determination, can get on pretty well in this world to-day, but one day they have to leave it all behind and go on to face God and the life to come." She paused a minute but he waited for her to continue. "I believe that God wants us to find out about Him and His love for us in this life, so that we are able to live in His Presence when we leave here. Surely it is more important to get to know God than just to get to the top of the tree down here?"

"And what do you call 'God's Richest Blessing'?" he asked her quietly.

"The knowledge of sins forgiven and peace with God through the death of His Son, Jesus Christ," she replied simply.

There was a long silence while Linda tried to get on with her work. Then, suddenly, Mr Stapleton pushed back his chair and rose to his feet.

"I think you are probably right," he said. "I'm going to see if I can visit my wife now, but I shall think about what you said."

He picked up his hat and left the room, and Linda sent up her thanks that she had been given the courage to witness once again.

# CHAPTER FIFTEEN

FOLLOWING the accident in the factory, Linda found that she and Richard saw a great deal more of each other than before.

At first it was the casual greeting at the Friday Club, but later it became obvious on the outings they had that he would always be at hand when she and Joan were together and, on joining them, would keep them amused with his lively and amusing conversation.

Everybody liked Richard and Linda stubbornly refused to believe that he had singled her out for special attention. After all, the three of them had the added interest of working for the same firm and, on several occasions, they had met together for the express purpose of discussing the possibility of starting some kind of Fellowship in the factory as a means of witnessing to their friends.

"We must pray about it first," Joan had said wisely. "We don't want to start something and have it peter out and belittle the things of God. If we pray on I feel sure we shall find more supporters and then we shall have a working nucleus on which to build."

"It would help if we had someone more senior to back us, too," Richard replied. "If only . . ." he added, spreading his hands wide and shrugging his shoulders. "Never mind, promotion will come when it is the right time for it."

The following week the three of them met again and Linda teased Richard:

"Taking over the factory yet?" she said, with a laugh.

"That'll be the day!" he replied. "No fear. I was chalked off properly this morning for putting through a special order when the boss was out. He told me I was getting too big for my shoes," he told them with a rueful smile.

"Nonsense," Linda stuck up for him loyally. "I'm sure you are as capable as any of them. Don't you think so, Joan?"

But Joan ignored the whole conversation as if she had not heard a word.

It was not until the next meeting of the Friday Club that Linda knew why. Entering the hall, she saw Richard standing on the platform, obviously looking for someone among the crowd of young people. He saw her almost as soon as she saw him and leapt down to the floor, beaming from ear to ear.

"Have you heard? Has Joan told you?" he asked her, eagerly clutching her by the arm.

"Heard what?" she asked.

"About me? Oh, do come over here away from the others." He led her over by a window.

"It's happened," he said and laughed excitedly. "I'm to be promoted. Mr Stapleton sent for me to-day and said that various members of the staff were being sent down to the new branch and that he intended to put me in charge of my department as a full manager! Isn't it wonderful?" He leaned forward impulsively and clasped her hand.

"Richard, I'm so very glad," Linda answered with real feeling. "I hope you will go on and do very well indeed."

Suddenly she realised that he held her hand in his and gently but firmly withdrew it and turned to include Joan in the conversation as she crossed the room to join them.

"Have you heard about Richard's rise in the world?" she asked, and Joan laughed.

"Of course I have. It was all discussed a couple of weeks ago at the Board meeting."

"You are the limit, you girls," Richard grumbled playfully. "Next you'll be telling me you knew, too, Linda."

"No. I hadn't heard a thing, and this discreet old owl wouldn't open her mouth and tell a soul," she laughed with Joan.

At work things were much as usual in the office. They were still very busy and kept on the go all the time, and Linda was relieved that it was so. She felt disturbed at the eagerness Richard had shown to tell her of his step up and tried to forget that brief moment when their hands had met. She found herself keeping a wary eye on her companions at the lunch-break, in case she was left alone and found herself in an embarrassing position with Richard. However, things soon became normal and she put it all out of her mind as a fleeting impulse.

"The quarterly stationery delivery from the wholesalers is generally checked and put away by my secretary," young Mr Stapleton told her one morning. "I don't think you were here when the last consignment arrived and Miss Cornell did it."

Linda put down the papers she was sorting.

"Are you warning me that a delivery is due to arrive

soon, sir?" she asked with a smile. The whole morning
had been a succession of phone calls, visitors, complaints
and other interruptions and her desk was littered with
papers on all different subjects.

"As a matter of fact I saw the lorry drive in when I was
coming over from the factory," he told her with a smile.
"Any moment now the phone will ring and someone will
give you a whole afternoon's work with the brief sen-
tence, 'The stationery has arrived, Miss Lewis!' "

"Thank you for warning me, sir," Linda said, and re-
doubled her efforts to tidy the mess in front of her.

Sure enough, scarcely ten minutes later the internal
telephone buzzed loudly. Linda picked it up and smiled
grimly as a voice announced at the other end:

"The stationery has arrived, Miss Lewis." That was all,
just the few words Mr Stapleton had used, but they
certainly upset her plans.

Down in the receiving room she found it hard to
believe that so much paper and so many pencils and
envelopes and elastic bands and such-like things could
possibly be needed in a factory of that size. But evidently
they were as she soon found on checking through
previous deliveries and looking at the depleted stocks in
the cupboards.

On returning, at last, to the office she was surprised to
find the senior Mr Stapleton sitting there in earnest
conversation with his son. At first she backed out again,
but they called her to come in.

"Don't go, Miss Lewis, we want to talk to you," the
Managing Director said, and she felt funny inside in case
she had done something wrong.

H

"I was saying to my son that there have to be some changes here now that the amalgamation has gone through," he explained. "We now have the other factory and its subsequent expansion or failure entirely as our responsibility.

"For some time we have known it would be necessary for my son to move down there and take over as soon as things were straightened out. Well, that time has come and very shortly he and his family will be moving to a nice little house they have had built ready for them."

Linda's face fell but she said nothing.

"My father was asking me what I intended to do about a secretary, Miss Lewis," the younger man continued. "And the long and the short of it is that I should very much prefer to take my own. But it is asking rather a lot."

"You mean me, sir?" Linda asked in astonishment.

"That's right. I have found you most dependable and efficient and it would ease my burden tremendously if you would come down, at least for a time, while I settled in in the new surroundings. It would be too awful for words if I had a complete stranger managing my affairs at a time like that."

Linda didn't know what to say. It had been fun visiting the new branch and spending a few days there; but to stay? That was a very different matter.

"May I have time to think it over?" she asked at last. "It is rather a big decision to make straight away."

"Yes, yes, of course. Let me see, it's Wednesday to-day: how about a decision by Monday one way or the other," the older man suggested, and so it was left for the time being.

Linda could hardly keep her mind on what she was doing for the rest of the day, and it was with real relief that she hurried to catch up her friend Joan when the afternoon ended.

"What do you think I ought to do?" she asked when she had told her all about it.

"It's a wonderful opportunity," Joan commented. "If I were you I would pray about it and then sleep on it, and then discuss it thoroughly with your parents in the cold light of early dawn at breakfast to-morrow."

"I think I will."

"What about Richard, will you see what he thinks?" Joan asked her suddenly and Linda flushed.

"No, I don't think so. I will tell him, of course, but whatever I decide has nothing to do with him."

"Perhaps not," Joan replied cautiously, but at the same time, she wondered.

In the end it was left entirely to Linda. Her parents rightly pointed out the advantages and disadvantages of such a step, but left it to her to make the final decision.

Richard said nothing, but, for the first time since Linda knew him, he took no part in the Friday Club and excused himself early and disappeared.

Linda herself, and her sister Mary, too, both prayed very much that she might do the right thing, and it was not until the Sunday evening that Linda made up her mind after reading the last chapter of Matthew with its final promise, "Lo, I am with you alway, even unto the end of the world." It seemed to assure her as a proof from God that she would not be alone if she went away.

And so it came about that a month later Linda found herself in strange surroundings, among people she had not met before and living in a hostel run by the firm for all the new people who came to the factory.

Mr Stapleton no longer had to be defined as "young" to prevent muddles with his father, for now he was the General Manager in charge of the firm and very keen to prove his ability.

Linda inspected the office and smiled. Instead of a rather elderly building, everything was new and clean and smart. A public address system had been installed to contact Mr Stapleton when he was in the factory and, on her desk, there were four telephones instead of the two she had used before.

It would take some getting used to, she was sure of that, but perhaps not as much as life in the hostel. Here she had a cubicle with all her possessions round her, and she was only separated from her neighbours by plaster board partitions seven feet high.

Feeling rather lonely and wondering whether she had done the right thing, she set off as soon as she was free and found a keen church. The very next day was Sunday and her choice proved better than her wildest dreams. A great crowd, many of them young people like herself, attended the morning service and she was accepted among them at once.

Perhaps it would not be so bad after all.

# CHAPTER SIXTEEN

As work at the new branch speeded up and a big advertising campaign began to bring in new orders, Linda found she had her work cut out to keep up with the everyday things which had to be done.

One day, when they had been particularly rushed, she tackled Mr Stapleton.

"It's no good, sir," she said. "I cannot catch up with all there is to do. Some duplicating, which ought to be out in a day or two, hasn't been touched. Could I, please, have someone to help me so that I can delegate some of my work."

"Of course, Miss Lewis," he agreed. "You are so quiet and efficient I'm afraid I had not noticed how busy you have been. By your manner anyone would think I was the easiest man in town to work for, and I'm sure that can't be true!"

Linda did not comment on his last remark, although she felt pleased that he was satisfied with her work.

They talked more fully about the prospect of a junior secretary and Linda was detailed to go over to the Labour Department and ask them for help.

All this took time and the day had passed before she had nearly finished her work, so she stayed behind and worked on alone before leaving for the hostel.

She was tired and had missed her meal, so she felt very

hungry as she left work. It was at times like this that she wished she had stayed at home.

Entering the hostel she crossed the hall and glanced in the letter rack, hoping for news from home. But there was nothing there with her mother's large writing on it and she was about to turn away when she saw her name. There, on a plain white envelope, she read, "Miss L. Lewis", in a handwriting she had never seen before.

Slipping the letter out of the rack she made her way wearily to her cheerless cubicle and let herself in. She took off her coat and hung it up and then leisurely combed her hair. Then, seating herself in the little arm-chair provided, she slit open the envelope and unfolded the letter. It was not very long and she turned it to see the signature, still puzzled. There it was, gazing up at her, Richard L. Thomas. Richard! Linda looked up unseeing out of the window and her cheeks coloured. Richard had written and, she couldn't understand why, but it gave her a warm, happy feeling deep down inside to hold his letter.

There was very little news and it was almost dis-appointingly polite and formal, but Linda felt a different person all of a sudden. She tried to convince herself that it was the contact from home which had cheered her up, but underneath something tremendous had happened and she knew in her hearts of hearts that it was not just the news but the writer which mattered.

A few days later Linda was working away busily when there was a knock on the door.

"Come in," she said, and a small, fair-haired girl entered shyly.

"I was told to come and see you by the Labour Department," she said, advancing to Linda's desk. "I've been doing junior work for six months in the Staff Department but was told to come over here this morning. My name is Audrey Naylor."

"Sit down, Audrey, and we will have a talk," Linda told her. "I want someone to help me who will do my copy-typing for me and sort out and file any papers that are not in use at the moment. Someone who can take a message on the 'phone accurately and run messages round the different departments. Now, tell me, how do you think you would qualify for that kind of work?"

She listened carefully as Audrey replied and was impressed by the clear way she expressed herself.

"Would you be willing to work late occasionally and put the efficiency of the office and firm before your private recreation?"

"Yes, Miss Lewis, I'm sure I would," Audrey replied earnestly, and Linda felt she would be just the kind of helper she needed.

"Well, suppose we give you a trial?" she finished. "Then we shall see what happens. If you turn out to be trustworthy and helpful and, above all, conscientious at your work, then I will train you so that you can deputise for me, and, who knows, one day you may be in my place interviewing a 'junior' for yourself?"

Audrey joined Linda the very next week and turned out to be all that she could have asked for.

They worked together well and Audrey lifted many of the everyday tasks from Linda which made the work less harrassing and more enjoyable as a result, and Linda soon felt quite at home in her new surroundings.

The church was a great help too and welcomed her among its members as if she had lived there all her life. Later Audrey began to go along with her and the two of them spent many hours at the services and Bible Study groups.

But, somehow, something was missing, and bit by bit Linda came to realise what was wrong. At first, when she had received a letter from Richard it had been a great joy to hear from such a great friend, but, as the weeks drew into months, the tone of the letters changed. Whereas the first one had been devoted entirely to church and factory news and all that was going on, the later letters began to include personal news as well.

Linda scarcely realised what was happening until she found herself skipping through a letter to find out how Richard was himself before going back and reading it properly for tit-bits about her friends.

Joan wrote frequently, telling her how much she was missed and how she, Joan, felt at a loss for a Christian friend in whom she could confide.

One day Linda received a letter from Joan telling her about a week-end conference to be held in a short while and saying what an interesting time they expected to have. Coming in in the evening, she found a letter waiting from Richard, also telling her of the conference and ending with the words, "It would make me very happy if you could arrange to have the time off to come and join us."

The following day Linda set out all Mr Stapleton's requirements just as she always did and then began to type some letters to special customers, but all the while she was hoping there would be an opportunity for her to ask about that long week-end. That morning she had made it a special matter of prayer that she might be guided as to what she should do.

Mr Stapleton arrived and the day's work began in earnest. First the post and then letters to take in short-hand, then the various engagements for the day. Everything was just as usual and continued until mid-morning when Mr Stapleton went round the factory to see that all was well, as he always did.

Before Linda had had a moment to speak of time off it was lunch-time and she knew that Mr Stapleton was meeting an important overseas buyer who would probably return to the office with him if things went well.

Evidently the talks over lunch were successful, because Mr Stapleton was not seen again until nearly three o'clock, when he arrived accompanied by another gentleman.

"Mr Fletcher is from Toronto and he thinks we may be able to do big business together," Mr Stapleton told Linda with a pleased smile. "He liked our new animated ads. and called me on the phone while he was down in Exeter on business."

It turned out that Mr Fletcher had a chain of stores in Toronto and surrounding districts and he felt something a little different would go down well.

"People like British goods," he drawled. "And I reckon if you could package some of your best goods in cute wrappings, we could push them across to folk by the hundred."

They talked about details for some time and then Mr Fletcher rose.

"I guess I must be going," he beamed, picking up his brief-case. "I shall look forward to hearing from you."

"We will send out sample packages as soon as we can get them designed and produced," Mr Stapleton assured him and Linda's heart sank. Bang would go her plans for a long week-end, she was sure. They were going to be far too busy for her to ask for time off.

Suddenly she heard Mr Stapleton speak to her.

"Where's your enthusiasm, Miss Lewis?" he asked. "You must be overtired. Let me make a suggestion." He leaned across his desk towards her. "How about two weeks flat out to make a good job of this order and then you can take a long week-end? Say Friday fortnight and the following Monday free and the firm will pay your fare home?"

Linda's eyes shone.

"That would be just wonderful," she exclaimed, realising that God had overruled and the week-end was hers and He had added still more by prompting Mr Stapleton to suggest a travel voucher.

For the next two weeks Linda worked as she had never worked before and cleared up all the odds and ends that were outstanding. She was filled with excitement and almost counted the days as they passed, and when eventually the week-end arrived it was all she could do to instruct Audrey in her work without letting her see how thrilled she was.

But, when she returned the following Tuesday she could hide her joy no longer for on her fourth finger, for all the world to see, was a beautiful diamond solitaire ring.

"Yes, Audrey, I'm engaged to be married," she told her simply and then the fun began.

The news spread unbelievably fast and congratulations flowed from all sides.

"I didn't give you time off in order to get rid of you," Mr Stapleton teased her. "Tell me, who is the lucky man?"

"Richard Thomas from a firm called Stapletons back at home," Linda replied mischievously.

"You mean young Thomas from our place, the new manager?" Mr Stapleton asked in amazement. "Well, you are a dark horse not to let on. At least you will be staying in the family, as it were. How long do you think you will be over here?"

Linda smiled.

"For some time, sir. We shan't be getting married just yet."

Very soon everything appeared to be back to normal except that many more letters arrived in the neat handwriting along with ones from Joan and her other friends who wrote to congratulate her.

"I must make sure you are ready to take over when I go," Linda told Audrey one day. "It won't be for some months, I don't suppose, but we ought to be prepared."

There followed many hours as she conscientiously instructed the younger girl in the use of the big electric duplicator, the addressograph and the adding machine they had recently added to their equipment.

"I know how to work the dictaphone," Audrey told

her, and Linda laughed and told her of the time when she
had wiped out most of the letters Mr Stapleton had
dictated.

She took no chances with Audrey and many times
found herself another job so that the younger girl could
take her place and become conversant with the different
machines.

"It's very good of you to bother," Audrey told her.
"After all, you could have let things go a bit now you
know you are getting married and leaving."

"And a fine sort of witness that would have been for
my Lord and Master," Linda replied. "Oh no, I feel a
Christian, or any other person, should do a job well no
matter what is going to happen."

At last the day came when Linda tidied her things for
the last time. She was hoping to slip away quietly, but it
was not to be.

"Mr Stapleton wants you in the canteen," Audrey told
her as the hands of the clock reached five.

"In the canteen? Whatever for?" she asked, but
Audrey did not reply.

If Mr Stapleton wanted her then she had better go. So
she hurried down the corridor oblivious of the fact that
Audrey was following with a twinkle in her eye.

Entering the canteen she found it full of people who all
stood up and clapped as she entered. Suddenly it dawned
on her what was happening, but it was too late to escape.

Mr Stapleton waited at the head of the room and all was
quiet.

"Miss Lewis, would you come up here, please?" he
said and went on as she joined him, "I want to assure

you, Miss Lewis, that we shall all miss your cheerful
efficiency when you are no longer with us, I in particular.
But it gives me great pleasure on behalf of all present to
give you this cheque as a gift for your wedding.

"May you be very happy indeed in the days to come
and may I personally wish you 'God's Richest Blessing'
as you once wished my son."

The clapping broke out again as Linda gave him an
understanding smile and there were cries of "speech" as
Linda looked down at a cheque for £15 in her hands.

"Speech!" they called and Mr Stapleton turned to her.

"You will have to say something, Miss Lewis; they
have all contributed toward the gift."

Linda stood flushed and confused and with tears of
happiness in her eyes.

"I don't know how to thank you," she began. "I've
loved being here and hope to come back and see you
again one day with—er—with my husband."

Loud cheers again filled the room and she stumbled out
blindly and away to catch her train.

She was on her way home—and to Richard.